Inheritance of Shadows

Lost in Time, Volume 0.6

A.L. Lester

Published by A.L. Lester, 2020.

Edited by: Lourenza Adlem
Cover Design: A.L. Lester
Image(s) used under a Standard Royalty-Free License.

ISBN: 9781393312246

For more information visit allester.co.uk[1]

Table of Contents

INHERITANCE OF SHADOWS

It's 1919. Matty returns home to the family farm from the trenches only to find his brother Arthur dying of an unknown illness. The local doctor thinks cancer, but Matty becomes convinced it's connected to the mysterious books his brother left strewn around the house.

Rob knows something other than just Arthur's death is bothering Matty. He's know him for years and been in love with him just as long. And when he finds something that looks like a gate, a glowing, terrifying doorway to the unknown, it all starts to fall in to place.

Matty's looking sicker and sicker in the same way Arthur did. What is Rob prepared to sacrifice to save him?

The answer is in the esoteric books...and with the mysterious Lin of the Frem, who lives beyond the gate to nowhere. It's taken Matty and Rob more than a decade to admit they have feelings for each other and they are determined that neither social expectations or magical illness will part them now.

A stand-alone 35k novella set in the Lost in Time Universe.

THANK YOU

Inheritance of Shadows began as *The Gate*, a free short story that I wrote quickly, to have something to offer readers as a taste of my work and my universe before *Lost in Time* was published. Although it finished on a satisfying note for me—Rob and Matty found each other—I found myself wanting to know more about what happened afterwards, so I began writing monthly episodes for my newsletter subscribers. This is the result. It includes *The Gate* as the first chapter, because it wouldn't make sense without it!

Very big, squishy thank yous go to: Lourenza for her encouragement in moving me along to self-publish; J.M. Snyder, as always, for her support, this time as a publishing partner; Jude Lucens, who provided some very necessary brain-storming that resulted in me losing 3,500 words that are now available to readers of my newsletter as *Rob's War*; and finally, all my newsletter subscribers, particularly those of you who took the time to let me know how much you were enjoying the serial. Plus my family, who wish their parent was more like the mother in *The Railway Children* "because she's still nice to her children when she's writing".

CHAPTER ONE: The Gate

June 1919

The road unfolded in front of the car as it ate up the miles in the night. Way above was the high arch of the night sky, as distant and cold and passionless as the afterlife he didn't believe in. Arthur was dead. Finally gone. After all these weeks, dragging from hour to hour, fighting for every last breath, he'd finally let go.

Matty didn't know what to do with himself, so he drove. Not to anything or from anything, it was an instinctive urge to keep moving. Before long he'd have to turn the car around and go back, back to the farmhouse; back to Arthur's cooling body, life drained and dignity finally returned. Not quite yet though.

Six weeks ago, he'd finally come back from France to find his brother sick. There had been no warning of it in his letters. Just the usual cheerful news about the neighbours and the cousins and the titbits about the grass in the top field starting to grow, finally, now spring eventually looked like it was coming in and they were thinking about sharing a couple of pigs this year with next door and what did he think? Nothing about the illness that must have been eating him alive from the inside even then, to be so thin when he opened the door. Matty almost hadn't recognised him. He was stooped like an old man and his skin was dry and yellow, stretched thinly over his face. Then he'd met Matty's eyes and Matty had drawn breath and stepped forward to put his arms around him.

"What's wrong?" he'd asked, without even saying hello. "Is it the flu? You said you'd got over it well!" Arthur had stepped back out of his grasp, held the door wide, and didn't answer until they were both seated at the kitchen table with a mug of strong tea.

"Doctor Marks can't tell me," he'd replied, brief and to the point as always. "Says it's a cancer, most likely, but she can't find anything specific." He'd poured a second cup of tea and that had been that.

In the night Matty had heard him pacing the floor of his room, talking in a low and urgent voice. The lamplight had crept under the door as he'd paused outside, wondering. When he'd knocked and asked in a low voice if everything was all right, Arthur had stood in the half-open doorway, blocking his view into the room; although over his shoulder, Matty could see the disordered sheets and crumpled pillows that spoke of disturbed sleep and troubled dreams, plus piles of the ubiquitous books.

Arthur had always been one for books. All through their childhood he had hoarded them like the dragons in his stories hoarded jewels, coming home triumphant from a trip to the library with yet another new volume. And later, when Father and the rector had helped him make the break from the farm and get a place at university with a scholarship, it had fed his appetite like dry twigs to a blaze. The house was full of them—Father had had quite a few of his own, even before Arthur had begun to add his share.

Now, after Matty's four-year absence, there were even more. The shelves were overflowing. Small books, big books, leather-bound, and cloth-bound. Hardcovers and paper covers. Rough-edged and smooth. Wedged in on top of each other, higgledy-piggledy, balanced in stacks on every available flat surface all through the house. Arthur was writing things down too—loose leaves of paper scattered around, notes stuffed into the middle of abandoned volumes in longhand and shorthand notation.

Matty had asked if Arthur was still writing columns—he had made a reasonable income with articles and stories for various papers and magazines in addition to overseeing the running of the farm—and Arthur gave him half an answer, purposefully vague. *The help on the farm had been down to one older man and a couple of boys in the last couple of years and it was hard to find the time. He found it difficult to concentrate since he'd become ill.*

When Matty pressed him to say when he'd first noticed his health had begun to decline, he wouldn't say. Matty bumped into Dr Marks in the village one day and she expressed the hope that Arthur was taking care of himself. She couldn't tell Matty very much about what ailed him; she thought it was probably a condition of the liver, but because Arthur was reluctant to let her look at him properly or be referred to a specialist, it was difficult to be certain. She was pleased Matty was home to look after him; they didn't see much of either of them around the village these days and they were both missed.

So Matty took himself back to the farm and tried to make things easier for Arthur. It was coming up to hay time and he worked long hours in the fields with the men to get it cut and stacked before the weather broke. He came home at twilight, itching and sore with exertion, but happy to be tired in a way that was easy to sleep off. The familiar rhythms of the farm settled into his blood again after four years of mud and bombs and gas and hurry-up-and-wait. Annie Beelock still tended the kitchen and the poultry, her son helped outside, and Gaffer Tom worked at the hedging and ditching. Jimmy and Rob both came home to their jobs as farmhands and that made it easier. Jim had his wife and family in the village, but Rob went back to sleeping in the loft over the far end of the ancient beam-and-cruck barn like he'd always done.

It was a small farm, but the years of war had meant that they had to work it hard and with efficiency, as the rest of the country had been worked to feed the army in Europe and the cities on the home front. His father had had a small private income before the war that meant they'd had the luxury of schooling and a touch of life outside the small farming community they had had inherited and Arthur had his writing. It felt good to be home.

Arthur though. Arthur was an enigma to him now. He'd always been the brother Matty looked up to. He was ten years older—almost too old to be called up in 1914 and anyway, reserved to work on the farm. He'd left for Oxford when Matty was eight and seemed even more god-like when he'd returned in the summers between classes. Matty had left school and worked with Father, content with the life of the farm and his round of friends and family. Arthur had gone to work on a

London paper for a while, but then come home and helped as well as working as a writer. After Father died, they'd continued in the same vein until Matty had joined up.

Now Arthur was changed. Not in the way so many men were changed, still able to hear the guns and smell the rancid, rotten odour of the mud. He was quieter, yes; but he was almost frenzied in his search through his books, focused on his work but unable or unwilling to tell Matty what it was he was seeking. He was thin and stooped and his yellowed skin had the texture of crepe.

He became weaker by the day after Matty returned until two weeks ago when he'd been unable to rise from his bed. He had begun wandering in his mind, agitated and upset, sending Matty, again and again, to make sure the gates and doors were shut, and the lamps put out downstairs. He had wanted Matty to promise to burn his papers and books once he was dead. Matty had baulked at promising any such thing, despite his insistence.

The end had come quite suddenly—Matty had been sitting in the faded red brocade chair by the bed, reading aloud in the afternoon sunlight, the familiar fall and rise of Dickens rolling from his tongue without really registering in his mind. Arthur had been lying on his side with his eyes sometimes open and sometimes shut, the cotton pillowcase stark white under his yellowed cheek. His breathing had been shallow but calm.

"Matty?" he had said. "Matty, I need you to get rid of the books. Keep the gates shut and get rid of the books. Promise me."

His eyes were huge in his thin face.

"Why, Arthur? What's so bad about the books?"

"I don't want you knowing," he'd replied. "I don't want you to have to go through this. I can't stop it now, I left the gate open too long, I thought I could control it. There's a line still clinging to me and I can't get free. Once I'm gone, they won't have a way in. Keep the gates shut, don't try to pull, and they won't have a way in. Burn the books, please."

And he had let his eyes fall shut again, exhausted.

Matty had taken his hand and sat and watched the sun move across the red flocked wallpaper that their mother had chosen twenty years ago, the dust motes dancing in the golden light. Arthur's breath had become shallower and shallower as the sunlight had become thicker and darker and golden like honey dripping off the spoon. As the twilight had fallen, the shallow breathing whispered away and everything that had made Arthur himself had left.

Matty sat and held his hand a little longer as the soft evening wrapped itself around them. Then he had straightened Arthur's limbs and closed his eyes and tidied him under the sheet. And then he had gone downstairs and out of the front door, closing it carefully behind him. He had cranked the starter at the front of the small car he had bought a couple of weeks ago, an indulgence he'd been embarrassed to reveal to his brother, and he'd opened the yard gate, got in the car, driven through and then got out again to close it behind him—and here he was, driving on the new macadam road up over the hills, head and heart quite empty.

THE FUNERAL WAS QUIET, solemn, nothing untoward. The rector spoke steady, kind words. Arthur was laid beside his parents in the small village churchyard, surrounded by countless generations of the same families who turned out to pay their respects. A pair of buzzards mewled close by on the thermals and Matty could hear a lark high above in the distance. The sun was warm on his shoulders as the open grave exuded the cold of the dark earth on his face. He scattered the first handful of damp soil on to the coffin and the hollow echo rang in his ears as he stood and watched the others who followed his example.

Afterwards, Mrs Beelock put on a high tea in the formal front parlour. Plates of thickly cut ham sandwiches, boiled eggs, the dark, rich fruitcake that she turned fresh from the tin. She and her daughter, Emily, circled round with the large teapots they used for the harvest festival, pouring endless cups of strong brown tea and milk chilled from the dairy slab with the cream still thick on the top. Conversation was quiet and unstilted. These people had known both of them all their lives. Understanding words; memories of shared boyhood; a hand pressed to his arm in passing by women who had been friends with his mother. Eventually, they all left. Mrs Beelock cleared and washed up and shepherded her daughter out of the back door to feed the poultry and go on home.

The house rang with silence. The men had gone back out to milk.

He sighed.

In the three days since Arthur had died, he hadn't really thought very much. He'd gone on with the farm work, he'd taken turns sitting at the side of the light oak open coffin in the formal front parlour, a fat, sweet-smelling beeswax candle at the head and foot. He'd eaten the food that Mrs Beelock put in front of him and taken his turn at the stone sink, washing the dishes as he always had. He'd slept in his bed in the room with the green wallpaper when it was time and woken up as he always did when the sun touched the picture of the boat in the gold frame that hung on the wall at the foot of his bed.

He'd been discharged and arrived home at the end of May. The long, hot, hard blue days of June had crept into the softer dog-days of July as he'd read volume after volume of Dickens to Arthur with slipping voice, seated in the red brocade chair with his feet on the faded rug beside the bed.

He'd asked no questions and Arthur had provided no answers. But now, here in the shabby back sitting room, it was just him and the books.

He poured a glass of brandy from the bottle at the back of the sideboard. The glass of the oval mirror behind was age-spotted and silvered and the heavy cut crystal of the brandy snifter was dusty. He wiped it out with the end of his black tie, uncaring. It tasted as it looked, aged and smooth, full on his tongue and hot in his throat. It brought him back to himself a little.

He sat in Arthur's chair, a dark, worn, comfortable leather club affair to one side of the fire, and gazed into the flames absently. He'd come home because he had never thought of going anywhere else. The farm was in his blood, as it had been in their father's and their grandmother's before him. He couldn't see himself existing anywhere else in the long term, especially after his time stuck in Flanders mud. He knew Arthur had felt the same. His relief when he'd arrived home and announced he'd left London permanently had been palpable. Arthur had needed more than the farm and through his studies and his writing he had got it. The land was secondary to that.

For Matty it was the opposite—he'd enjoyed learning at school, he enjoyed reading, discovering things. He had realised that he liked to visit new places and meet new people, so long as they weren't trying to kill him. But for him, that came second to the land. They'd complemented each other well, fitting together like two pieces of a jigsaw, understanding each other, working around each other and carving out satisfactory lives.

Of course, the war had changed that—it had changed things for nearly everyone. Matty wasn't naïve enough to think that life was going to go back to exactly how it had been five years ago. The little car standing outside was one of the signs that changes were still happening. For all of that though, he hadn't thought he would be navigating the changed world without Arthur to make him see things from a different point of view.

He picked up the book at the top of the pile on the floor by the armchair. It was large, and leather-bound and heavy, with rough-cut pages and bits of paper in Arthur's neat hand sticking out from between them as bookmarks or notes. Idly he opened it. It was well-thumbed. It fell open at one of the pages Arthur had marked.

It was in a language he didn't immediately recognise. Latin? Looking closer, it wasn't Latin—he had learned at school—it was in an archaic form of English. Handwritten in thick cursive, with notation and diagrams. It looked like someone's diary or a book of notes. Arthur had added his own, on the paper he had slipped between the pages.

Tried salt across door and window frames and around edges of room, no good.

Smell of burning oil.

Push back. The energy follows thoughts.

They can hear me thinking.

Cut the line.

Matty stared at the page thoughtfully and sipped some more brandy.

THE TAP AT THE KITCHEN door took him unaware and he took the bottle of brandy out to answer it. It was Rob. Matty stepped back in silent invitation and let him in. "All right?" Rob asked, quietly.

"Not really. Do you want a drink?" He gestured to the bottle that he'd set on the table.

Rob looked at him with narrowed eyes and nodded. "I'll join you." He'd been promoted up to sergeant in the Signal Corps, Matty remembered, in a disconnected sort of way.

"Come on through. I was in the sitting room." Rob hesitated. The farm men never came any further into the house than the big, busy kitchen for meals. That and to use the bathroom out beside the scullery. But it was an unusual day. He followed Matty across the flagged passage and into the comfortable sitting room. In front of the sideboard, Matty slopped some more out of the bottle into another dusty glass and proffered it. Rob took it and sat where Matty gestured, on the wide, worn leather settee. Neither of them spoke. It was a comfortable kind of silence.

He and Rob had always got on, in the way of single men. They'd gone to the pub together sometimes and taken a couple of local sisters on courting walks through the bluebell woods as a pair, a long time ago. Matty hadn't been particularly interested in Marie Booth and he didn't think Rob had been much interested in her sister Clemmie, either, and probably for the same reason. Matty had made sure never to look at him *like that*, though. He didn't need that sort of trouble on his doorstep. Now though. He really looked at the other man, comfortably sprawled opposite him. Looking back, they'd been inseparable. They'd spent every moment they could together.

Four years of muddling through in the trenches and taking soldier's comfort in a few minutes here and there, furtive and messy behind the lines had snapped something in Matty. He didn't really care overmuch what people thought of him, not anymore, and he suspected that a lot of other people were the same. When you'd had boys too young to be away from their mothers die in your arms, you learned to grasp for any comfort or happiness when it appeared and damn the consequences.

Rob had noticed Matty watching him. "I was just checking on you," Rob said, quietly, misinterpreting Matty's stare. "I can go if you like."

"No, don't go. I appreciate the company. I just haven't got much talk left in me."

"No need to talk with me, Matty, you know that." Rob's smile was slight, but genuine. He turned to small talk. "Cows are milked. I left the churns in the dairy, though. It's too warm to put them out tonight. We'll need to do something about the back of the barn before the winter. There's gaps of light coming in through that red stone wall. The brick's crumbling away."

They made desultory conversation for a half hour and Matty's eyes started to droop. "You need to sleep, lad." He could hear that small, genuine smile in Rob's voice.

"I do." He stood and put his glass on the sideboard. "Thank you, Rob."

"Any time, Matty. You only have to ask. Whatever you need." Rob stood quietly beside him, stalwart and solid and so immensely comforting. They were facing each other. Rob raised his hand to the back of Matty's neck and Matty stepped forward into the embrace. Rob's other arm came around him and settled him, forehead against that broad shoulder, smelling of hay and good sweat. It was such a god-damned *relief* to have someone else take his weight for a little while. Neither of them moved. After a little while he felt Rob press a soft kiss against the top of his head. He was hard in his corduroys against Matty's hip and Matty felt himself stirring in response, but neither of them acknowledged it. "Get some sleep." Rob's voice was low and calm. "It'll all look different in the morning." He let his arms drop away with a passing caress to Matty's nape and they stepped apart.

AFTER THAT, THINGS settled into a routine. There was no doubt in his mind—or anyone else's—that Matty was back to stay. They worked well as a team, him and Jimmy and Rob. There was no recurrence of the day that they had embraced in the parlour. They watched each other, but neither of them took it any further. It was a grieving time for Matty, and he didn't have it in him to start anything.

He didn't stop himself looking quickly enough, though, the day he went into the tack room at the end of the barn searching for Rob and found him stripped down to the waist and washing in the rough stone sink. He pulled himself together sharply, but he also saw that Rob had noticed him noticing, and had looked back. He let himself admire a bit, then, on the quiet.

They were harvesting, rushing to get all the fields cut before the weather broke. It was nice, watching Rob's shoulder and back muscles ripple as he tossed the stooks of corn up on to the top of the touring steam-powered threshing machine when it was Webber's Farm's turn to have it trundle into the yard. When he caught Rob watching him in return, he simply smiled. It felt good to have this small secret between them. It wasn't safe, of course. But it felt good. Nothing might ever come of it. It very rarely did, in Matty's experience. Only shared looks and being scared to take it any further.

So, he was surprised to find Rob knocking on the kitchen door one evening in September. The nights were starting to draw in, despite the long, hazy days of summer that were still clinging, and it was dimpsy outside. The run of clear skies had broken with a steady drizzle that thrummed down onto the red dust of the farmyard turning to mud.

"Evening, Rob," he said, as he moved back to let him in through the door.

"Matty. Thanks." The other man stepped over the worn stone threshold and turned to hang his drenched coat and cap up as Matty closed the door behind him.

"What's the matter? Is there something wrong with the cows?" Matty busied himself pushing the kettle onto the hob of the range.

"No. No. Nothing like that." Rob stood by the table, one hand in the pocket of his corduroys, his free hand absently fingering Arthur's papers that Matty had spread out all over the scrubbed wooden surface.

"Sit down. The kettle's nearly boiling. Tea?"

"Yes, please." He didn't sit, just propped a hip on the table. Matty moved around steadily, measuring out the tea into the pot with the square, silver caddy-spoon, waiting until the kettle was rumbling before he poured the boiling water onto the leaves. He brought it over to the table and cleared a space among all the papers to set it down, then turned to get a couple of heavy mugs from the wooden drainer; and then fetched the milk jug from the cold-slab in the larder.

He put it all down and sat opposite Rob, who finally pulled out one of the ladder-backed oak chairs and took a seat. "What's the matter, Rob?"

Rob watched him, eyes cautious and assessing over the mug of tea, the slight steam obscuring his quiet brown gaze a little. He gestured to the papers, rather than answering. "What's all this, then?"

Matty thought for a moment. He didn't *not* want to talk about it. But it seemed crazy when he thought about explaining it someone else. Finally, he said, "Arthur. It's Arthur's work. I've been trying to make sense of it all."

Rob pulled a sheet toward him. "It's not in English," he observed. "What language is this, then?"

"I'm not sure. Some of its Latin. Some of its old English. And some of it...I'm simply not sure. I wondered if it was Arabic, or Chinese or something." He was trying to categorise the loose papers by language and possibly by who had written them. He recognised Arthur's neat, crabbed hand.

A lot of the writing on the loose leaves was his, but there were others too. It was difficult to tell because of the different languages and alphabets. There was no consistency. "I was trying to work out what he was working on when he got sick. It doesn't seem to make much sense, though. Lots of talk of gates and keeping them shut. He was extremely worried about it the week before he passed." Matty swept a hand over his forehead. "I couldn't reassure him, because I didn't understand him. And he couldn't explain it. He was raving for a lot of the time."

Rob looked at him sympathetically. "I heard he was seriously sick for quite a while before any of us came home?" The burr of his country voice was gentle. "I'm sorry, Matty. I should have said before. I didn't really know what to say, though, it seemed like it all happened so sudden-like. And then the corn needed getting in before the weather broke and we've not really spoken."

Matty studied his tea intently. He didn't know if he could bear sympathy, even now and even from Rob, who knew him as well as anyone. "I didn't know," he confided. "Not 'til I got home. He didn't tell me. It was so *peculiar*, Rob. He wouldn't see Doctor Marks after she told him she thought it was cancer. But I don't think it *was* cancer. Not the way he was raving at the end." Rob cocked his head quizzically. He bit his lip and considered his next words. Matty could see him wondering if he should speak. "What?" he prompted. "Come out and say it, whatever it is."

Finally, Rob seemed to make up his mind to speak. "There's something peculiar at the back of the byre," he said. It wasn't what Matty was expecting at all and he frowned.

"What sort of something?"

"Something I think you should see." Rob put his hand over Matty's, where it lay on the table. It was big and warm and rough from the harvesting and Matty liked how it felt. "It's...odd."

"Odd how?"

"Odd. I can't explain it without showing you." He withdrew his hand and Matty missed the warmth. "Come on."

THEY PUT ON THEIR GEAR and went out into the drizzle. The dusty yard of the summer was clumping into mud under their boots and Matty didn't like its greedy suck. It was better around the back of the barn. The cattle were making their soft, comforting noises inside, munching and rustling in the dark with the occasional snorted punctuation.

"Here. Round the side." Rob slowed as they approached the corner. "Don't get too close. I don't think it's safe."

There was a lamp lit at waist-height, with the glow spreading warmly from where it was hanging. But it wasn't a lamp, when he looked properly. It wasn't anything. It simply *was*. He glanced at Rob. His face was illuminated on one side by the golden light. "What is it?" Matty asked him.

"I don't know. It's just...light. I walked around it and you can't see it from the other side. I walked up to it and tried to look past it. I think..." his voice wavered a tiny bit, "...I thought, I could hear some sort of noise coming from it. Singing. Crying. Something." He glanced at Matty and looked away, embarrassed at his own fancifulness.

Matty swallowed nervously. Rob was steady. He'd always been steady. Neither of them were given to fancy. That had been Arthur's job. He took a step closer and peered at it. Around the light there was a shimmer, almost like a heat haze. It went out a few feet in each direction to about the size of a door or... "A gate," he said. And looked at Rob.

Rob looked back. "That's what I thought, when you said." His voice was calm. "I came to tell you about it, and then, you told me that." He swallowed. "I can hear someone the other side. Voices." He went to step forward and Matty put a hand on his forearm.

"Let me." He took another step forward and another. It was three or four yards away. One more step and he could hear what Rob had heard. Faint singing or crying. He couldn't hear clearly enough to say which. He turned to look back at the other man. "I can hear it."

Rob stepped up to join him, shoulders pressed together, and they took another two steps side by side. Matty reached out a cautious hand and touched the shimmer around the edges of the glow. It seemed to flow toward his fingers, a delicate blue-white light, and he pulled his arm back, quickly.

"All right?" Rob's voice was quiet.

"Yes. It's cool. Not cold. But definitely cool. It feels prickly. Like a shock from electricity." Rob stretched his own fingertips out and shuddered a little as the light seemed to jump out and meet them. He dropped his arm and the blue glow retreated, like ripples stilling in a pond.

The noise got louder. It was a keening, singing sound. Almost like hounds giving tongue, Matty thought. They stepped back as simultaneously as they had stepped forward. As they did so, the light at the centre brightened and expanded. It pulsed in time with the rhythm of the voices on the other side. They retreated further, almost back to the corner of the barn. The light expanded and became almost impossible to look at. Mindful of his eyes, Matty half-closed them, watching through his lashes. The keening song became so loud that he put his hands over his ears and saw that Rob had done the same.

Suddenly, both the song and the light disappeared. Snapped off at their apex. Floating on Matty's retinas though, was the silhouette of a figure outlined against the burning light. He blinked the floating image away rapidly and felt Rob tense up stiff as an ironing board beside him.

"Who are you?" he heard Rob say in a hard voice—his sergeant voice, as Matty always thought of it. His eyes cleared and in the dim drizzle he saw that there was, indeed, a man in front of them.

He was crouched on the ground in the continuing rain, braced on his arms, gasping great gulping breaths and retching. There was something strapped to his back. A pack? Matty blinked frenziedly and wished his night vision back.

Rob obviously hadn't been as blinded as he had been and had stepped forward, putting his stocky body between Matty and the intruder. "Who are you?" he repeated. "What's going on?" Matty went to step up beside him and Rob put an arm

out, pushing him back again. "No," he said. "Stay back, Matty."
Matty paused at the command in his voice.

"I'm fine." He pushed the sheltering arm down and stepped
forward. "Who are you?" he echoed Rob. "What's happening
here?"

The drizzle lightened, and the silhouette became clearer as
Matty's eyes adjusted. The man was vomiting properly now. He
had a plait of long hair falling over his shoulder. Matty took another step forward and whilst the man's position didn't change,
it immediately became clear that the approach was unwelcome.
He felt hands on his shoulders. "Don't go any closer." Rob's
voice was deep in his ear.

"It's all right." Matty wasn't sure which of them he was reassuring. Rob, cautious and grounded; the vomiting visitor, or
himself. Rob squeezed his shoulders and let go.

"Do you need help?" He stepped forward again and Rob
followed him.

The man turned a pale face up toward them, pushed the
long tail of hair back over his shoulder, and wiped his mouth
with the back of his hand in the same motion. He stared at
them and they stared back and after a moment, he pushed himself back onto his knees.

Matty realised with a start that it was a pair of crossed
swords or sticks on his back. He had a bag strung across his tor-
so crosswise, like webbing to hold bullets.

They all stared at one another for a moment longer and
then the man leaned forward and retched again, muttering
something as he did so. That was it. He needed help and obviously wasn't a threat. Matty knelt beside him, disregarding
the weaponry, and put a hand on his shoulder, pulling the plait

back from his face. The vomiting fit went on for some time and Rob eventually came up to his other side. Matty could see that he was debating whether to take the swords out of their scabbards whilst the stranger was incapacitated. They shared a look over the man's back and mutually decided not to.

Eventually the retching stopped, and the man sat back on his heels again. Matty handed him his handkerchief and he wiped his mouth with it and went to offer the soiled cloth back. Then he glanced at Matty, who said, "Keep it," and pushed it back toward him. It was stowed in a jacket pocket. The rain worsened at that point and Rob said, "Let's get him inside. It's not going to stop."

They each put a hand under the man's shoulders. He seemed to understand what was happening and helped them pull him to his feet. He paused, panting a little and letting them take his weight. He cleared his throat and said something that might have been 'thank you', but Matty didn't understand the language. "This way," Matty said, gesturing toward the house at the same time as Rob said, "Let's get you inside, lad."

He was wearing a leather jerkin, Matty realised, as they made their way unsteadily around the corner of the barn, into the main yard. It was keeping the worst of the rain off. The mud was worse on the way back across the yard, the accumulated dust of the summer now a sucking, soupy mess that reminded him of the trenches. He sometimes thought he wasn't ever going to be comfortable with mud again. A definite issue for a farmer. At the kitchen door, the man baulked, like a horse put to a too-tall fence. Rob stepped ahead and opened it, stepping in and taking his coat and cap off, whilst Matty said, "It's all right. Come in out of the wet." He encouraged their visitor forward.

Eventually he took a tentative step across the threshold and Matty followed him into the warmth and light of the kitchen. Rob was pumping the lamp; and it flared up, illuminating the room and their inadvertent guest, who was gazing around curiously. Matty hung up his wet clothes as Rob poured a glass of water and offered it to the stranger. "Here, drink this. You were desperately sick." The other man took it and sniffed, cautiously, then sipped.

"Thank you," he said. His voice was soft, and his accent was peculiar. "I mean you no harm," he added, haltingly. "The gate..." He paused, head tilted as if he was listening "The gate was... protected. Guarded," he corrected himself. And then he sneezed.

"Sit, sit down," Matty insisted, suddenly aware of how awful the stranger looked. His face was pale and his lips blue tinged; and he was starting to shiver. Matty pulled out a kitchen chair and pushed him down onto it. His knees buckled and he went down all at once, looking queasy again.

"I apologise," he muttered. Matty met Rob's eyes over his head. Rob nodded toward the kettle.

"Let's get your wet things off, lad," he said, using his kind sergeant's voice this time, as he moved to help do just that. Matty put the kettle on the hob and turned back to see Rob wrestling the weapons and bag off the young man's shoulders. And he *was* young, Matty could see now, in the better light. He was tall and skinny, with a thin face and blondish-brown hair that was further darkened with the rain. It was coming out of the plait and he kept pushing it back behind his ears. The leather jerkin came off to reveal a shirt of some sort of linen material underneath, that was at least dry. Rob hung both the jerkin and the scabbard up on the pegs behind the door as if he did that every day, ignoring the young man's protests. Matty proffered the warm towel that hung on the rail in front of the range, and he passed it over his face and then scrubbed at his hair, before combing it back with his fingers.

"What's your name, lad?" Rob asked, taking the towel back.

"Lin. My name is Lin. Of the Frem." He paused and tilted his head again in that listening motion and spoke stiltedly. "The gate. It will open again. I have to close the gate." He gestured to his belongings. "I need my things. I thank you for your help. I need to do it now." He went to stand, but Rob pushed him back down as Matty made the tea and passed the mugs. Lin of the Frem took his, despite his protestations, cautiously wrapping his hands around its warmth. He took a sip and twisted his lips before taking a proper mouthful. Matty sat down at the other side of the table.

"And so, Lin of the Frem, what are you doing here? What was that light? And what do you mean, about a gate?"

Rob was quiet, but he meant business. He stood close behind the other man and wasn't going to let him rise without some answers. Matty could see it from the set of his shoulders and the way he leaned against the rail of the range, arms crossed. Lin seemed to realise that he wasn't being given any quarter, either. The lamplight chased across his face, and Rob's. Lin looked sharp and soft in turns; Rob looked intent. His eyes flicked to Matty's across the waiting space of the room. "The gate..." Matty murmured softly. "What does that mean?"

Lin tilted his head again and looked at Matty. "Your brother." It was as if he was tasting the word. "Your brother knew about the gate?"

Matty blinked, startled. "Yes. Yes, I think so. His writing ..." He gestured to the piles of papers. "He wrote about a gate. About keeping it shut." He swallowed. "Was that what we saw just now? What is it? Where does it go to? Where are you from?" He felt like a fool. The man had appeared out of empty air. Except the air hadn't been empty, it had been filled with light.

Lin took another mouthful of tea and shook himself like a dog. It was a visible gathering of his wits. "I came through the shimmer to try to stop the break. There is a break in the shimmer, yes?" He watched them both, seeming to will their understanding. "I need to mend it. It is dangerous. You must let me go."

"Is that what we saw?" Rob asked. "The break in the shimmer? Like a door?"

"No. That was the gate that the Ternants opened to get me through here. But there is also a break in the shimmer, a *thinning*. Yes. I have been tasked with closing it. But it was guarded on the other side and I couldn't do it. My kias was not strong enough." He tipped the mug and drank more tea. You have to let me go and try again." He was looking better and better, recovering quickly.

"But..." Rob was cautious. "Where are you from? What is the shimmer? You weren't there and then you were. I know what I saw. You saw the same, didn't you, Matty?" He wasn't sure what he'd seen—his gaze at Matty wasn't as certain as the tone he was aiming for. Matty stood and went over to him, putting a hand on his arm.

"Yes, I saw the same. He came from nowhere. And I heard the song and saw the light. What was the singing, Lin?"

"It was the Ternants, trying to open the gate for me. It was extremely difficult." His speech was becoming clearer and faster. "I am to mend the thinning in the shimmer that is being worked on by the Ternant's enemies. They fear that those who have opened it are going to hurt your people here. You, the Delflanders."

"Hurt us how?" Matty was starting to wonder about Arthur.

"Steal kias. Some of you have some kias, although not as much as our own people. They can drain it away and use it for themselves. It will kill you if that happens."

Matty and Rob looked at each other.

"My brother. Arthur. He died. He told me to shut the gate." Matty pointed at the stack of papers at one end of the table. "He collected all these books and papers. They don't make much sense to us." He included Rob in his gesture. "He withered away. The doctor said it was a cancer. He died telling me to keep the gate closed. Can you tell me what happened?" He felt his heart rate increase.

Rob put a hand on his shoulder. "Steady, Matty."

Lin put the mug down on the table decisively. "I have to go back. I have to shut the gate. I will explain afterward, but you must let me go." He stood, and Rob and Matty both stepped back as he moved toward the coat-pegs. He reached for his jerkin and shrugged it on, making a distasteful moue at the cold, damp leather. He glanced at them both before reaching for the swords. "I mean you no harm," he stated again. "But I must do this."

He slipped into the harness with the agility of one who did it every day, and they let him. "I thank you for your help," he said. And opened the door and stepped out.

Matty looked at Rob. Rob looked back. As one, they moved toward the open door. Rob grabbed the tilly-lamp off the kitchen table in passing. It was full dark outside now, not simply the dimpsy-dark of the end of a drizzly late-summer day. Lin was rounding the end of the barn.

They could hear the sound again. To Matty, it seemed more of a screeching wail than a song, now. The light was leeching a cold blue around the corner and they slowed as they ran up to it. Lin had drawn his swords and stood in a fighting stance in front of the light, which was brightening as they watched. They could see a shadow in the centre of it. They both jammed their heels in as they came up behind Lin, one on either side. The sound was ear-splitting and there was a hot, harsh breeze coming from the centre of the light. It smelled of the desert.

"What is it?" Matty had to raise his voice to be heard.

"It is a carnas. A creature. They want to send it through to hunt. We must stop it." Lin looked very young and extremely fierce as he shouted back, voice carried away by the increasing wind. He shoved his swords at Matty. "Here. Hold these." He dug into the bag that he had re-slung over his chest. Matty watched the gate with one eye and Rob with the other. Rob still held the lamp, low in front of him. He was watching Matty, not the gate.

Matty knew, suddenly. All the glances, all the touches, all the exchanged smiles this summer and early autumn. They meant something. Rob was back to stay and that was all right with him. He grinned a determined grin across Lin's head and raised the swords. Rob raised the lamp.

"When I say," Lin shouted. "When I say, throw the lamp. Hard. If it gets any further, we are lost. It will take more than me to capture it if it gets all the way through." He gripped handfuls of something-or-other from his bag. Some kind of soil or crumpled leaves. Matty didn't have time to look. The shadow was becoming more distinct and the screeching song was unbearably loud now. He wanted to drop the swords and put his hands over his ears.

"Now!" Lin flung the soil-stuff at the distorted silhouette in the centre of the light. You could clearly see it was some sort of animal. "Now! Do it now!" He was shouting. Rob came alive with a yell of his own and bowled the lamp after the soil-stuff. There was a god-awful noise. Screaming, yelping, munitions going off. Matty crouched down and put his arms over his head.

Then silence.

He drew a few breaths and slowly uncurled. The other two men were also lying in the mud. They were both blinking.

"Is it gone?" Rob's voice was heavy and the way he pulled himself up was heavier. He extended a hand down to Matty and Matty grabbed it to help him rise. Lin pushed himself to his feet beside them.

"Yes. It is gone. It will not return. Thank you." Lin busied himself collecting his weapons from Matty and wiping the mud off them.

"But what was it? Who are you? What happened?" Matty looked at him. "Is that what killed my brother?"

"Perhaps?" That odd, bird-like tilt of the head again as Lin stared at him. "Yes. Yes, I think that is likely. I am sorry. The Ternants did not realise what was happening until now and we acted as soon as we could. He had kias, yes? He worked?"

Matty stared at him blankly, rain running down his face. "I don't know what that means," he said, flatly.

"He had a book, did he not?" More staring and head-tilting. "A book of notes. You must destroy it, Matty. Destroy it. Do not read it. You do not have kias. You must not follow this path. It is dangerous for you. For both of you. For any of your people." He turned his gaze on Rob. "You must not let him pursue this. It must be prevented."

Rob stared back at him. "I can't stop him doing anything, lad. You've got the wrong man."

Matty glanced over at him and their eyes met before he dropped his gaze to his muddy boots. "Let's go in," he muttered. It was still drizzling.

"I must go back," Lin said. "Remember what I said. You must not follow this path. Please?" He stepped away and stretched his hand out. Blue light began to gather around it. Matty looked at Rob again and they both stepped back. "I thank you for your help, both of you." He made a sweeping gesture with both arms and a pool of blue-silver light appeared to spring from his fingertips. He stepped into it. The light shrank to a pinpoint and both it and the man were gone.

Matty blinked and turned his gaze to Rob. "What just happened?"

"I have no idea." Rob stretched out his hand so that his fingertips touched Matty's and Matty gathered his courage along with his breath. "Will you come inside with me? We can look at the papers and talk about it?" His grip was warm on Matty's palm despite the mud as Matty drew him closer. He didn't loosen his grasp as they walked across the yard side by side.

CHAPTER TWO: A Culmination of Years

"What just happened?" Matty asked again, as he dropped Rob's hand to shut the outside door.

"I honestly have no idea," Rob repeated. He took his coat off automatically and hung it on the hooks in the little scullery. "That was an elf, wasn't it? Or a fairy?"

Matty coughed. "Erm. Yes. Or perhaps we're both going mad?"

"At the same time? Unlikely." Rob moved to the range and slid the kettle onto the hot plate. Matty was freezing. He always looked a bit peaky, in Rob's opinion, but now he looked cramped over on himself, as if he was about to come apart.

"Come here," he said. He reached out a hand to the other man and leaned back against the rail of the range as Matty took it, drawing Matty toward him. "Come here," he repeated. Matty stepped close, chest to chest, and Rob wrapped his arms around him. Matty slid his arms round Rob's waist, hands flat on his back. The range-rail was warm against his lower back and Matty's hands were cooler on his shoulder blades.

"You're freezing," Rob said.

"Yes." Matty shivered. "I can't seem to get warm at all, these days." He laid his head on Rob's shoulder, hair damp against Rob's neck, and Rob held him tighter, sliding a hand up to cradle the back of his head.

He'd wanted this for as long as he could remember. He knew himself tolerably well these days and he'd realised a while back—in the middle of a bombardment at Vimy Ridge in the spring of 1915, in fact—that Matty was the one he wanted. He'd been in Rob's periphery for years, so long that Rob had failed to realise that, actually, he wasn't at the periphery at all, he was at the centre of everything. He'd decided then and there that if he ever got out of the mud and got home, he'd make sure Matty knew he was at the centre and take what came.

Whatever was going on here, with Arthur dying and lights and elves and Matty looking peaked, Rob was going to sort it out and make sure Matty was all right. And if Matty wanted Rob around after that, then that was grand. If he didn't...well, Rob would cross that bridge when he came to it.

He wrapped his arms more tightly round Matty, leaned back against the range a little more, and spread his legs to take more of the other man's weight.

After a little while, Matty stirred against him and said, "Rob," his voice low and muffled by Rob's collar. Rob pressed him even closer and Matty burrowed his nose, still not quite as warm as Rob's skin, in against his neck, right above the top of his collarless shirt. His breath was much hotter than the rest of him, hotter than Rob's skin.

Rob swallowed. He hadn't meant this to be more than comfort, hadn't meant to start anything. And now something was starting, all by itself.

"Matty?" he said, diffident question in his voice. Matty was hard against his hip and Rob was stiffening.

Matty gave a little sigh in response and drew back a bit to meet Rob's eyes. Rob's gaze dropped to Matty's mouth. Matty smiled a small, secret smile. "Now?" he said. "We're doing this now?"

"Looks like it. If you want?" Rob slid the hand still on the back of Matty's head down and round to cup his jaw and run a thumb over his lips. They were full and soft, and he'd thought about doing this for years. Matty's smile grew under his touch. Rob reached behind him with his other hand and dragged the kettle off the stove top.

"All right, then," Matty said, and leaned forward to press his mouth to Rob's. Rob's thumb fell away. Everything fell away.

There was only soft and hot and wet and silky and his tongue slipping into meet Matty's, not battling exactly, but neither of them giving any ground. It was perfect.

Matty's arms around him were tight and Matty's body against the length of his was warm and muscled and everything he'd wanted for the last decade and a half. He cupped Matty's face with both hands, holding him where he wanted him, and Matty moaned into his mouth, arms tightening.

It was quick after that. Fumbling with each other's buttons and drawers, getting his hand round Matty's prick, feeling Matty's hand on his own in turn, exploring that silken, hot, hard length. Matty drew both their cocks together in one hand and Rob wrapped his own hand over the top. Matty drew back to watch, and they both looked down, foreheads pressed together as they came with gratifying simultaneity.

"God," Matty exhaled. "That's made a mess."

Ever practical.

"Hang on, I've got a hanky." Rob delved deep into a pocket. "Here." They cleaned themselves up as best they could, unspeaking, and then Rob drew Matty back into his arms. "Come here," he said. Matty took up the same position as before, but he was warm now, and relaxed.

"God. I needed that," he said. "I've needed that for years."

"Yes," Rob said. "Me too. Stupid to have waited." He turned his head and met Matty's mouth again. They kissed some more, long, languorous, luxurious kisses without the urgency of before. Although Rob could feel himself hardening again, it was without the frantic need to take his arousal any further.

Finally, Matty drew back and took his hand. "Come on," he said. "The fire'll still be on in the other room. Let's sit."

Rob followed him into the sitting room, and they settled themselves on the overstuffed sofa. There were piles of papers all around and Rob was jolted out of the haze of tenderness and underlying arousal and reminded of what had happened earlier.

"A gate?" he asked, looking at Matty.

"Yes. That's what it says. Look, here," he said and pulled a medium-sized, leather-bound green book toward them from the low table in front of the sofa. It was the one that Rob had seen before, with all the different handwriting and languages. "He wrote in the margins... Some of it seems to be translation, but some of it is commentary." He pointed to a particularly illegible and cramped section of marginalia. "*Difficult to open, but almost impossible to shut*," he read out. "*Creature, carnas? Same?*" He turned the page. "This is what's scaring me, though.

It fits with what Lin said. I think it's a translation. *Open the gate at your peril, once they know you can do it, they will drain you.*"

He lifted his brown eyes to meet Rob's. "Arthur was raving about being drained and shutting the gate. Cutting a line. If we're not going mad and this evening happened, then that seems to back up what Lin said. Something from *through* the gate had got its claws into him and was making him sick." He paused. "And I think it's got its claws into me, Rob. I've felt awful the last few weeks since he died. I don't know what's wrong with me. I'm exhausted. And cold all the time."

He stopped talking. Rob stared at him. He couldn't find any words and his mouth was dry. Eventually he said, "But that Lin...he said it was gone."

"Maybe it is. Maybe I'll start to feel better now. Whatever that was...that we saw in the light...it looked like a monster. Surely we'd have noticed if there was one here?"

"Maybe not," Rob held out a hand and when Matty put his own in it, drew him closer, tucking him against his side. "I'm not saying I believe in magic, mind. But that, this evening? It wasn't anything I've seen before. And all these books. Your brother was up to something, man. If we're not going mad together, then this evening happened and maybe Arthur wasn't raving after all." He paused and then decided to say it. "And, Matty, I could *feel* what was going on. When he made the light and suchlike. It *pulled* at me. I could feel it. Like...like the percussion wave when a shell goes off? But backward. It felt like it was pulling me."

Matty drew away a little from his sheltering arm and looked at him. "Pulled at you?" He made a face and leaned toward the book on the table again, leafing through it. "Pulled.

Look. Here." He pointed to a page and shoved it toward Rob. "It talks about *pulling*."

Rob leaned forward next to him, thigh to thigh, and read where he pointed. It was in English, written with a dip-pen by the look of it, in careful, flowing script that was reasonably easy to read once you'd made out the quirks of the handwriting. He'd left school at thirteen like his peers, but he liked to read and the lending library in town was well funded. He thought of himself as a self-educated man. He traced the first line with his forefinger. "*Gather the kias from your surroundings. From your partner or partners. Draw it toward you. Pull it in. And then use it to link to the border and pull from that. You will start to see the light gather at the point on which you focus.*"

He looked at Matty. "That sounds like what happened." He paused. "Matty. What's going on?"

Matty bit his lip in thought as he stared back. "I don't know. But that's what I've been trying to find out since I got back and Arthur was so sick. I don't want to go the same way. We need..." He paused. "...I need to find out what's going on and stop it. And maybe this Lin of the Frem can help me."

Rob put a hand on his knee. "We, Matty. Not just you. We."

CHAPTER THREE: An Elf-Shaped Elephant

Rob had gone back to his own bed after another hour or two looking through Arthur's books. They had kissed at the kitchen door, long and languorously, but passion had not sparked again in the same way. They were both tired and it had been a hell of a day. Rob slept in the barn, in the loft at the end. Before the war, the handful of unmarried farm men had often lived there. There were barracks-like beds above and in a small room partitioned from the barn at the foot of the stairs to the loft there was a stove, a table, and a few easy chairs. The men used the water closet and bathroom at the back of the scullery and came into the house for their meals. It was only Rob out there now, which was to their advantage.

"Tomorrow," Rob had said, forehead pressed to Matty's. "Tomorrow I'm going to lay you down on a proper bed and take my time with you."

Matty had grinned at him. "I'll look forward to it," he muttered, nipping again at Rob's stubbled jaw. "I've got to go to town in the morning. I ordered some leek plants from Simon Parker. I kept meaning to put seed in and never got round to it. I've got to pick them up."

"I'll help you get them in. I keep forgetting today's Friday. Is Mrs Beelock coming in?"

"No, she's been having the weekends off. Her arthritis isn't getting any better."

Rob shot him a vulpine smile. "All the better, then," he said and pressed a final kiss to Matty's mouth. "I'll see you in the morning."

THINGS DIDN'T LOOK any different in the morning.

MATTY WAS UP EARLY despite the exertions of the previous night. He had slept reasonably well, but he was tired. He was sitting at the kitchen table with a mug of tea and a bowl of porridge, staring blankly out of the window at the continuing drizzle, when Rob chapped at the door and let himself in.

"All right?" Rob said.

"Yes. More or less. You?" His response was reflexive.

Rob stepped over toward him and laid a hand on his shoulder, then after a little pause, bent down and kissed him gently on the cheek, before going over to the stove, helping himself from the porridge pan and teapot, and pulling out the chair opposite to seat himself.

It was a normal morning.

Except it wasn't.

"Yes," Rob answered him, the response so delayed that Matty had almost forgotten what he'd asked. "It was a quiet night after all that. The cattle settled and I didn't hear anything else."

"Me either." Matty took a swallow of his tea. "I slept all the way through 'til it got light."

"What time do you have to meet Parker?"

"I just said I'd see him in the morning. He was going to take the plants to the market for me and he'll be there until lunchtime at his stall."

"I'll help Jimmy milk and then turn the cows out into the top field. By the time you're back, I'll be ready to help you plant the leeks."

It seemed like they were having a normal conversation about normal things and ignoring the large, elf-shaped elephant lurking in the kitchen. Matty determinedly mixed his metaphors and grasped the elf-elephant by the horns.

"I want to go and have a look behind the byre," he said firmly, "and go through more of the books this afternoon."

Rob continued eating his porridge. "Good idea," he said. "I'll help. As much as I can anyway. I was going to re-stack some of the hay in the back byre, but it can wait. If you help with the evening milking, we can get it done in half the time and then we can come back and carry on reading."

Matty swallowed uncomfortably. "You're distinctly calm about it all."

Rob looked up and met his eyes for the first time with a grimace. "Bloody hell! If you think that, you don't know me as well as I thought you did." He rested his licked-clean spoon on the edge of his blue-and-white Devonware bowl and reached for his tea. "I'm trying not to panic." He gave small, thin-lipped smile that lacked humour. "I've met frightening things before, Matty, but I *understood* them. They were logical things to be afraid of. Bullets. Shellfire. The wire. But this... I don't know what it is, only that it's something I don't understand. It's scaring the daylights out of me inside, even if I'm not showing it," he said and drank some of his tea.

Matty looked down at his own mug. It was nearly empty. "Sorry," he said. He swallowed the dregs, but continued to hold the cup in his hand, taking comfort in its lingering warmth. "I'm out of sorts."

There was a pause.

"Well," said Rob. "Yes. Not unreasonably." He stood up and put his bowl in the sink. "More tea?"

"Please."

Rob brought the pot over to the table. He poured another cup for each of them and then seated himself again, opposite Matty. He picked his mug up with both hands and leaned back in his chair, stretching his legs under the table until they tangled with Matty's. Matty picked up his own mug and smiled at him.

"It's going to be all right, isn't it?" he asked.

"Which part?" Rob smiled back at him.

"I'm not sure." Matty smiled back, unable to stop himself. "You and me? I think that's going to be all right. Isn't it?"

Rob didn't break eye contact as he answered, slowly. "You and me? It's something I've wanted for a long time. I'd like it to be all right." He looked down into his mug, placed it on the table, and ran his finger round the lip. "I've not been with many people. Many men. A few, in France." He looked up again and met Matty's gaze. "No women, not really. Even before...before I went away."

"What about Clemmie?" Rob had been walking out with Clemmie Booth in a desultory way, the same as Matty had been walking out with her sister Marie.

"Clemmie? No. We're good friends still. She wasn't ever looking for a husband. I think she was only walking out with me to stop her father trying to marry her off to someone else. She's a telegraph clerk now, you know. Over in Salisbury. She joined the Auxiliary Corps. She wanted to get out of the village, make something of herself. Old Man Booth wasn't going to let that happen without a fight."

He hadn't been keen on educating his daughters. "What about Marie? Do you hear from her? We exchanged a few letters at the beginning, but after I went forward, we lost touch."

"Not directly. Clemmie and I write sometimes. She says Marie is going to stay in nursing. She doesn't much want to come home either."

The older Booths had an isolated upland farm further along the hill from the Webbers. Mr Booth had only allowed the girls to walk out with Matty and Rob because Matty's mother had gone and talked to Mrs Booth. She'd felt sorry for the girls. He'd certainly been put on notice that if he put a hand on either girl, not only would Old Man Booth be after him, but so would his own mother.

"Just take them about a little bit, dear," she'd asked Matty. "They're only allowed out on a Sunday to church."

Matty had liked both Clemmie and Marie. But not in the same way he'd liked Rob.

"I'd like it to be all right between us, too," he said again, aloud.

"Then it will be." Rob was definite. "The other... I don't know about that. We need to find out what Arthur was doing." He drank more of his tea and then cautiously asked, "How are you feeling this morning?"

"Better than I have done. It was a relief to sleep." He rose from the table and started swilling out the porridge pan and crockery. "Let's get going then. Once we've got the outside work done, we can see if we find anything in Arthur's papers."

Rob stood too and started drying the bowls with the tea-towel from in front of the range. "You've been looking by yourself all this time. Perhaps a fresh eye will help."

"Perhaps. I'm so sick of it all. And last night... I'm scared too, Rob. I'm a rationalist, for goodness sake! I don't even really believe in a god anymore. And that...last night. It wasn't rational."

"No, it wasn't. But we both saw it and heard it. It happened. So, whatever it was, it was real." Rob hung the last mug on its hook and turned toward Matty, taking his hand and drawing him closer, wet hands from scrubbing the saucepan and all. "Come here a minute." He arranged Matty comfortably against him and Matty returned his embrace, resting his forehead on Rob's shoulder. "We'll get to the bottom of it, lad, don't fret." He ran his hands up and down Matty's back as if he was soothing a nervous horse. "Try not to think about it for now. Let's get things done and come back to it later. Perhaps we'll have a different angle on it."

Matty huffed a laugh and drew back. "I'd welcome that. I feel like I've been banging my head against a brick wall. Come on then." He reached for his coat and cap. "Let's go."

THE SCENE OF LAST NIGHT'S drama was a let-down. There was nothing out of the ordinary there except the faint traces of Lin's vomit. Matty didn't know what he'd been expecting. An elf-shaped hole in the universe? A tidy fence painted white, with a snicket gate labelled *Enter here to solve your mystery*? There was nothing particularly out of the ordinary that he could see, only the churned-up ground.

"I didn't really expect there to be anything peculiar here," he said, flatly.

"No, there's nothing to see," Rob answered, poking at the mud desultorily with the toe of his boot. "I can feel something though. I think. That sort of pulled-all-ways feeling you get sometimes before thunder? Do you get that?"

"I know what you mean. I can't feel anything."

Rob hunched his shoulders. "I can't really explain it any better than that." He put a hand out, stretching toward the place where Lin's gate had been. There was a clear line on the ground. On the one side of it, the side they were standing on, the soil was churned and disturbed with the marks of their not-quite-fight. On the other side, it was smooth and undisturbed. "It tingles. And it's a bit tacky. Sticky." He stretched out further, tentatively, palm toward the exact place the light had been. If it had been a gate, he would have had his hand flat on its surface. "I can feel a sort of resistance. Almost as if there's something there that I can't see. But not really." He stepped forward and pushed his hand further, with no visible resistance.

"Did you see that?" He turned to Matty.

"No? What was it?" Matty had been watching, but he hadn't seen anything at all.

"A bit of light. Very faint." Rob drew his hand back and repeated the sweeping motion. "Same thing...it's a flickering glimmer. Almost where the air feels thickest..." He paused. "Sorry, I'm not making sense."

"No, it's all right. You are. I just don't think we understand it at all." Matty bit his lip. "Do you think the gate thing is still there?"

"Maybe? I'm not sure." Rob stepped forward, deliberately crossing the demarcation line in front of them. Matty reached out, too late to stop him.

Nothing happened.

"There's nothing here," Rob stated, unnecessarily, turning toward Matty again, hands back in his pockets. He stared at the ground and stirred it some more with the toe of his boot. "Nothing at all."

They stood in glum silence for a moment or two before Matty said, "Let's get on then. Maybe we'll find something in the books to make sense of it all."

LEEKS IN THE GROUND and cows milked, they made thick sandwiches of bread, butter, and jam and settled in the parlour as the clock was chiming six. It was dull outside and Matty lit the fire, more for its cheer than because it was cold. The low thrum of desire between them sang in a subdued tone, the anticipation that later they would be going to bed with each other.

Matty kept catching himself watching Rob in the deepening twilight instead of concentrating on the book he'd pulled at random from of the pile on the floor. Rob was sunk deep in the leather club-chair, absorbed in whatever he'd found, sleeves rolled up to his elbows, collar undone, an incongruous pair of spectacles perched on his nose.

"I didn't know you wore specs," Matty commented, without really meaning to say it out loud.

Rob put his finger on the page to mark his place and smiled as he looked up. "Not long had them to be honest," he said. "I started to get headaches when I read, so I thought I'd better see about it. It's helped quite a bit."

He looked back down at the page. "I might have found something here," he said.

Matty rose from where he'd been sitting on the settee and went over to perch on the arm of the chair. "What is it?"

Rob leafed back a few pages. He had picked a journal by the look of it. It was a brown leather book, worn and well-handled to softness. The ink was faded on the cream pages, but the script was beautiful, and easily understandable. "It's written in a couple of different hands. Look, you can see. There's this one, at the beginning—" He leafed further back. The writing changed to a smaller hand that made Matty think of an older person. "Some of it is in English...some sort of travel journal, I think. He's talking about India and the Himalayas. Kashmir, Ladakh. And then sometimes he writes in some sort of code." Rob leafed forward again. "Look, here," he said and pointed to the page.

There were letters, but not in any language Matty recognised, and it wasn't the beautiful, small, neat cursive of the previous page. The letters were separated out into a grid of columns and rows. "What is it?" he asked.

"Don't know. But it's not a proper language, is it?" Rob was hesitant. "It looks to me like some sort of Trench Code."

He'd been in the Signals, Matty remembered again. "Can you crack it?" he asked.

"Perhaps, given enough time." Rob smiled at him again. "I'm not overly good at it, though. If Arthur couldn't do it..." His voice trailed off.

"He hadn't had any training," Matty said.

"I haven't had any training. Only what I picked up from my captain while..." He abruptly stopped talking and bit his lip. Matty looked at him, waiting for him to continue. There was clearly a story there, but it was up to Rob whether he wanted to tell it or not. "Anyway," Rob resumed. "Maybe. I can have a go. But although that's interesting, it's not the most interesting thing. Look, here." He turned the pages forward again to where he'd been reading when Matty disturbed him. "Here, the hand changes. See."

He pointed to the page. This hand was a larger cursive. Still fluid and beautiful, but completely different. It wasn't as legible as the earlier one. "He says that his father has died and he's using the book to continue his record of 'Pater's search'. There's drawings. Temples, maybe? And a map of what he says is a cave system. It's hellishly creepy."

"Let me see?" Matty reached out his hand and Rob handed him the book. It wasn't large, but it was thick. He turned the pages forward and backward, as Rob had been doing, so that Rob could still see them.

"There," Rob said, stabbing with a blunt finger at the text. "It says he's found the caves again and he wants to go back and explore them. That he can *feel the pull.*" Matty could hear him italicising the words. And here..." he turned the page, "...here there's a sketch-map."

It was difficult to make out the tiny labels on the map itself. It did look as if it could be a tunnel system. Matty peered at them. "Give me your glasses," he said, absently, and Rob placed them in his outstretched hand.

"I couldn't make it out," he said. "Maybe take it over to the window?" The lettering was faded to a pale brown, but in the better light by the south-facing windows, Matty could decipher a bit more.

"It some more detail about the map," he said. "*Rough, steep, up, down,* that sort of thing. And here..." He traced with his finger and realised Rob was looking over his shoulder, "...here it says *border weak, pull strong.* Where it opens out into this bulb-shape, look."

Rob took his glasses off Matty's nose and put them back on his own, peering closely at the page. "Yes, I see. Well," he said and drew back. "That's helpful I suppose. A border, the pulling thing. We're on the right track, anyway." He stepped away, back toward the chairs. "Have you found anything?"

"Not really. I'm still looking at the really old one, with all the different languages. Do you think that could be in code as well?"

Rob frowned, thinking. "I didn't think so when I saw it...but I wasn't really expecting anything like that. Let me have another look."

They sat down together on the sofa and Matty picked up the embossed green book from where he'd put it on the floor. He handed it to Rob, sliding along the settee so that they were pressed thigh to thigh. Rob's thigh was warm. As he took the book, he turned his head and smiled at Matty. Instead of taking the book out of Matty's hand, Rob kissed him. It was a slow, soft press of Rob's lips to his own, unhurried and affectionate, with their fingers entwined on the gilded cover of the book. It seemed to Matty that it was an action without expectation, a declaration of Rob's position. Here they were, together. Rob wanted to kiss him. He wanted to kiss Rob. And so, Rob made it happen.

That seemed to sum up their relationship, from way back when. Whatever Matty needed or wanted, there was Rob, facilitating it. Quiet, persistent, and consistent. Steady and steadfast.

Matty took his other hand from the back of the settee and cupped Rob's jaw. Rob gave a little noise in the back of his throat that Matty interpreted as approval, so Matty started kissing him back. He hadn't had a lot of practice at kissing, but what he *had* done, he'd liked. He softened his lips and drew back a little, then drew his mouth across Rob's. Then he pressed firmly but gently, close again. Rob's breathing was speeding up, as was his own.

Rob drew back and smiled at him. "Do you want to look at this now? Or do you want to go to bed?" He dropped tiny, tender kisses along Matty's jaw, from his chin up to a place under his ear that made Matty shiver.

"Erg," he said, intelligently. "We should keep going…but bed sounds extremely good." He took a turn at mouthing at Rob's stubble, that made Rob draw in an extra breath.

ROB HAD NEVER REALLY slept in another person's arms. They had fallen asleep as the last of the light faded out of the September day, the curtains open upon the trees and hills behind the house, satiated and laughing at stupid jokes and word-play, with his head on Matty's chest, Matty's arms around him. It had been nice. Right.

He woke instantly, as he was prone to do these days, instantly alert. It was starting to get light, and so must be about half past five. He found himself thinking that they'd need to get on and see to the milking, get it out of the way before going back to the books. Jimmy had Sunday off, so he and Matty usually did it together. He pushed the thought out of his mind and focused on the legs entangled with his own, the hip beside his, the low, regular, slight snores coming from the man he was in bed with. Rob was lying on his back and Matty was on his front, buried like a piglet in the straw with the grey woollen blankets and the feathery quilt up round his ears.

He turned on his side, rolling closer and stroking a hand down Matty's back and inadvertently poking his hip with his hard-on. Matty was wonderfully warm.

"Morning," he said, nuzzling at Matty's ear.

Matty made an undefinable grumbling noise.

Rob continued his exploration of Matty's hairline and the back of his neck. He'd discovered last night that it made Matty wriggle in an uncommonly appealing fashion.

Finally, he got a reaction.

"Hhhhrumph. Geroff," Matty said, exploding in a tangled flail of limbs as he rolled away, laughing. "Stop it, you bastard!"

Rob followed him, laughing too, as Matty rolled on to his back, pinning him pleasurably chest to chest. Matty had quite the impressive hard-on to match his own.

"Morning," Matty said, finally, meeting Rob's eyes and smiling. He thrust his hips upward a little and Rob mirrored him, maintaining his gaze and lowering his face to kiss him.

It quickly turned heated. They thrust together in symphony, slick-sliding together and moaning into each other's mouths. Finally, Rob couldn't maintain his breathing, thrusting, and the kissing all at once. He drew back a little and concentrated on watching his lover's face. "Come on," he whispered. "Come on, Matty, I want to see you. You're close, I can feel it."

Matty came with a quiet, pained gasp, and Rob followed him over. He tucked his forehead down to Matty's shoulder and Matty tightened his arms around him. Suddenly, he felt a wave of emotion. "I think I'm in love with you," he told Matty's shoulder, quietly.

Matty nuzzled him, where his neck and shoulder joined. He didn't answer for longer that Rob was comfortable with and as the hot flush of embarrassment washed over him Rob began to tense, ready to pull away. Matty tightened his arms. "No, don't, Rob. Don't go." He was silent for a moment longer. "I'm in love with you, too," he said, softly and sincerely, right in Rob's ear. "I've been in love with you for years. I didn't go on all those walks with you and the Booth girls because I wanted to court them. I wanted to spend time with you." He swallowed. "And this summer. Since we came back. Since Arthur..." He paused again. "I think about you a *lot*, Rob. So. I'm in love with you too." He squeezed Rob tighter for a moment and then relaxed, keeping Rob wrapped up close. "This has been a long time coming. And I'm glad it's finally here."

Rob relaxed completely, laid out on top of Matty, the sticky mess they had made sandwiched between them. "The cows," he muttered. "We need to milk. And I need a tiddle."

"In a minute. Rest here for a minute more."

Rob curled against him a little more and settled down. The cows could wait five minutes, as could visiting the lav.

CHAPTER FOUR: Breaking the Cypher

"I think I've got it," Rob murmured, one Saturday evening in November as they sat on either side of the fire in the parlour. He had a notepad on his knee and was transcribing from what Matty thought of as *the Himalayas book*, with the coded text and sketch-maps. It had been raining all day and they'd been hauling muck from the heap behind the byre to put on the fields of oat stubble. It had been a relief to come in and have a bath before they'd eaten, and they were now relaxed and tired.

Matty paused in his own reading to look over at Rob. He was still working on the green book himself, on the pages of what he thought of as *spells*. Some of them were in reasonably plain if old-fashioned English, some were in languages he could make a decent stab at with a dictionary, and a few were in a completely incomprehensible scrolling script that he couldn't place, even after two months of searching. "Got what?" he asked, intelligently, pulled from his fugue.

"The cypher. There's a bit later on, toward the back, that's a translation, I think. It looks like I might be able to make the rest out from there."

Matty rose and went over to sit on the arm of Rob's chair. He often sat like this, reading over Rob's shoulder as they puzzled out some piece of nearly indecipherable script. They were moving forward slowly with understanding what the books said. There were many others—piles of them all around the floor. Matty had ploughed his way through Arthur's well-thumbed edition of *The Golden Bough* and agreed with Rob that it was the biggest load of cobblers he'd ever come across, neither of them having much use for either magic or religion. There were history books, psychology books—Mr Freud was another load of perfect bollocks, Matty thought, despite Rob's interest—and books on different languages and people and places. As they had sifted through them all during the dry autumn, it had become clear that the focus of the collection was the pair of antique, handwritten books they had initially identified. Arthur had gathered the rest of his library in his quest to understand those. Now Matty and Rob had taken on his mantle.

Matty often wondered how long Arthur had been investigating this. Was it something he'd come across during his time in London? He'd gone from Oxford to work at the *Evening Trumpeter* when he'd gone down in 1897. He had travelled abroad to cover the war in the Sudan. He'd been to Afghanistan to write about the Pathans for the same paper. "Perhaps he picked up the brown book in India," he mused, out loud. "That would make sense, wouldn't it? A lot of the notes are about that area."

"Perhaps," Rob agreed. "I'm not sure it matters, though. Look at this." He pointed to an untidy page of writing on the flyleaf at the back of the book, scratched in pencil. It contrasted sharply with the reasonably neat pages of the rest of the notebook. He recognised the hand as the one filling the second half of the book. "Here, look, it's a translation of the cypher."

"I thought you said it was Trench Code," Matty asked.

"Sort of. It's a cypher, really. Trench Code is impossible to crack without a code book—you can guess, but really, unless you know what the words are supposed to stand for, you're stuck. A cypher, though. You can crack a cypher, if you're lucky. Even if you don't have the key." He drew his finger down the pencil-covered, discoloured page and Matty became a little distracted, following its path. "It's not a direct key, this here. But I think that it's a translation of an earlier bit of cypher. This one, here." He flipped back to a page much earlier in the book, a left-hand page, facing the map of the cave system on the right.

"Here, look. This grid here has pencil marks overwritten. Very faint." He pointed. "And I've just realised...the first few letters on *this* page..." he flipped back to the flyleaf at the back of the book, "correspond to them. Which gives us somewhere to start." He grimaced up at Matty. "I'm kicking myself. I've been thrashing through it for weeks and not getting anywhere, and it was here all the time. It looks like someone tried to rub them out on the first page, once they'd written it out in longhand."

Matty looked. "Yes, I can see the marks. So, what does it say?"

"Good question," Rob grinned at him. "I thought it was a description of the cave system to start with, but it's not. It's not connected at all, I don't think. Look, here." He traced the pencilled script, faded with time and spelled out slowly...

"I am sure that it was a Hollow that killed my beloved Lucy. I saw its eyes in the firelight as it ran. These creatures that come through the gate in the border are evil in both their manner and in the way they inhabit the bodies of men, women, and even children and animals by the pernicious and twisted use of their shimmering magicks. Their draining of the energies of the body is bad enough. I sometimes wonder if they have their designs on me, although I am fighting it well enough if they have. The most brutal thing about them, however, is this hollowing out of a living body as a host and replacing the soul with a vile creature that wishes only to rapine and kill."

"That sounds...pertinent," Matty said.

"Yes. I thought so." Rob grimaced. "This bit about the gate and a border. Do you think that's what Lin meant when he was talking about the shimmer?" He tapped the place on the page with his finger. "It sounds similar."

"It does. And the notes in the margins of this one—" Matty reached for the green book, "—where Arthur has scribbled things. It talks about a gate and draining people. And later on," he leafed frantically to and fro, "it talks about a border, I'm sure of it." He found the place he was looking for. "Here, look. *Gather the kias from your surroundings. From your partner or partners. Draw it toward you. Pull it in. And then use it to link to the border and pull from that. You will start to see the light gather at the point on which you focus.* That makes more sense if the border they're talking about is that thing Lin was calling the shimmer. There were lots of shimmery lights back in the summer." He pushed his hair back from his face. "I don't know, Rob. None of it really makes sense unless you suddenly start believing in the supernatural." He bit his lip.

"That's the thing, isn't it? I've seen a lot of crazy things in my time. And some damned peculiar ones at that. But this..." Rob left the sentence hanging. "This takes the biscuit."

They had both together and singly gone back to the place behind the barn over the last couple of months, looking for any trace of what had happened and seeing if the gate or Lin would reappear. There had been nothing. Life had settled into a calm, peaceful routine that Matty relished.

Plus, the Treaty of Versailles had been registered with the League of Nations late in October. Matty had felt an enormous sense of relief that the peace was formal now, signed and sealed by the high-ups. Fritz having to pay for all the damage he had caused everyone by sucking them into four years of war seemed only fair. That had been one of the topics of conversation when they had gone down to the County Cinema in Taunton with Mrs Beelock and her daughter a week before to watch the Pathé newsreel of the two minutes silence at the new Cenotaph in London.

However, it was a stunned, waiting, recuperating kind of peace for them both, Matty thought. He was reeling still, from coming home and from Arthur's death. Rob was gathering himself together almost visibly, losing that overlay of Sergeant Curland and returning full-time to Rob who the neighbours knew was a good man to ask for a hand with their hedges.

He could feel them growing again, on the cusp of moving forward. Rob spent his nights in Matty's bed in the house instead of in the barn. Annie Beelock only came in mid-morning now, her health needing her to rest, and it was a luxurious thing, this waking in the arms of someone he loved. They had fallen into it with ease and familiarity, eating whatever Mrs

Beelock cooked for dinner for all the farm men like they usually did, having bread and cheese and cake for tea once she'd gone, and washing up companionably together; and then settling in front of the fire with the books. They had fallen into a pattern that Matty imagined would be like being married. If men could marry the people they loved.

The war had shifted something inside them both. Coming so close to so much death meant that neither of them were inclined to waste more time. They saw what would make them happy and had grabbed it with both hands. That didn't solve the problem of the books.

Although, it wasn't really the books that were the issue. It was more that Matty was failing. Not as quickly as Arthur had, for whatever reason. He could feel it in his bones. It could have been no more than the normal slowing down of his body for the winter. But it wasn't. A glorious, dry, clear, and cold October had morphed into a bitterly cold November. It made him think back to the last autumn of the war, with the angels' wings of blue and gold arching with a kind of glorious, terrible disinterest over the ants of humanity crawling around in the mud.

He had the same feeling now. The bitter frosts, the clear blue skies of the onset of winter, made him feel like the world was waiting for something to happen. Watching him with a lack of interest that bordered on not noticing him at all. He was failing. He knew it and Rob knew it.

"What's to be done, then?" Rob had asked one Sunday morning in early October as they were moving the churns of milk out to the block by the lane where the carter would pick them up to take to the station. "I don't like the look of you, lad. And I don't want you to go west like Arthur." He obviously felt awkward bringing it up and had steeled himself to flank Matty with the question as they were working. Matty was getting tired more easily and he supposed that there was no hiding from Rob his diminished appetite and weight loss.

He launched the last of the churns up on to the platform and stepped back, taking his cap off, and wiping his brow with his sleeve. "I'm glad that's done. I like giving Jimmy the Sunday off, but it all takes longer."

"Jimmy's wife's got him painting the bedroom, he said. She took him out to buy the paint last weekend." Rob allowed Matty to prevaricate, but as they turned back to walk up the drive, he had put his hand on Matty's arm. "Matty. I'm serious."

Matty shrugged his hand off gently. "I know you are. I don't know. This was Arthur's enterprise, not mine. I run a farm. He was the brains."

Rob had looked at him long and hard. "Do you really think that?" he'd asked quietly. "Because you're wrong. You might have chosen not to follow the same line as Arthur, but you and he have the same amount up here," he tapped Matty's head, "however you choose to use it. So, don't give me any of that." He had returned Matty's solemn stare. "We'll work it out. I promise you. I've waited more than a ten-year for you. I'm not losing you to this. Whatever it is."

So, they kept on with the books.

Rob interrupted his brown study with an embarrassed cough. "About that," he said, seriously.

"About what?" His serious tone drew Matty's attention and he swivelled where he was still perched on the arm of the chair.

Rob pushed at him gently. "About the supernatural. Go and sit back over there."

Matty arched his eyebrows enquiringly but did as he was told. Sometimes doing what Rob told him to do worked out extremely well. He didn't really think this was going to be one of those occasions, but the thought did cross his mind.

Instead of moving toward him, or speaking, Rob sat still and looked at him for a moment. "Promise me," he started to say, stretching a hand toward Matty. "Promise me, nothing will change between us?"

Matty looked at him, brow furrowed. "What do you mean? What might change?"

Rob bit his lip and kept his hand extended, but he turned it over, palm up. "You know I said I could feel the *pull* that the book talks about?" He gestured to the spell-book Matty was holding in his lap. "That one, with the marginalia? And that it felt like a backward blast from a shell, when Lin was there?"

Matty nodded, silent.

"Well, I thought I'd see if I could do anything." Matty could see the hot tide of a blush rising in Rob's neck and he wouldn't meet Matty's eye. "I always fancied being a magician, when I was a kid. Dad used to tell me I could be one when I grew up." He smiled a tiny, secret smile. "I believed him, because you believe everything your father tells you as a kid, don't you?"

Matty nodded again.

"So, I *pulled* the stuff I could feel, like the book said. Then I focused and pushed it out. And...watch. I can do this."

He opened his palm, and in the centre, about an inch high and half an inch across, a small, translucent rose-coloured flame sprang to life.

Matty stared, blinking.

Rob closed his fingers in over his palm and the flame went out. Then he opened them again and after a second or two, the flame reappeared.

"So," he said, finally meeting Matty's eyes over his extended, flame-filled palm. "It looks like my Dad *was* telling the truth after all."

CHAPTER FIVE: Rob Impresses Matty

Matty stared at Rob. "That's...unexpected," he finally managed to say. He swallowed. "Um. Is it difficult?" The tiny flame sat in the centre of Rob's calloused palm, flickering gently. It didn't give off a great deal of light, about the same as a candle might if set against the background light of the fire. He leaned forward in his chair and reached out a hand hesitantly before glancing at Rob and asking, "May I?"

"Of course," Rob said. Rob was watching him rather than the flame. "It's not hot," he said softly.

Matty cautiously moved his finger closer, biting his lip. He wasn't scared exactly, but only a fool would be blasé. The flame wavered as he approached and then, as he touched it, it jumped like a candle in a draft and morphed around his fingertip, still on Rob's palm, but stretching out to meet him. It was cool and a little ticklish. Where he touched it, the colour changed from rose-pink to a sort of pinkish orange. He drew back and the flame followed an inch or so, before reforming in Rob's palm. Matty put his finger out again and circled it. When he was close enough, it followed the motion of his hand.

He looked up at Rob. "It tickles. What does it feel like to you?"

"Cool. Fluttering. Like a moth." Rob looked at his palm and then back up at Matty. "It doesn't upset you? That I've been practising without telling you?" He looked almost agonised.

"Not at all. Well. Perhaps. I'd have liked to have helped. But not really." He poked at the flame again, curiously. "Do you notice how it reacts when I touch it? Does it make you tired, doing it? What does it feel like to call it up?" He stood and shoved aside the table to kneel at Rob's feet on the thick fireside rug.

Rob curled his hand shut to extinguish the light and then opened it again. He breathed in steadily and then breathed out. Nothing as strong as blowing, simply a calm soft breath. The light sprang up after a few seconds. This time it was green.

"How did you do that?" Matty asked, poking it with his finger again.

"I thought about it. When I don't think about the colour, it makes that pink flame. If I want a different colour, I have to *think* at it. Not quite picture it." He pulled at his ear awkwardly. "That's not a very good explanation. I haven't got the words really."

Matty held his hand palm down over the flame. It was still free from heat. It flickered a little and drew upward as if it was reaching for him. He looked up at Rob. "What else have you tried? I know you, Rob." He smiled. "This isn't the only thing you've had a go at, is it?"

Rob blushed. "Erm. No. Not exactly." He shifted uncomfortably on the dark red leather of the armchair. "I wanted to try and open the gate. The one Lin went through." Matty flinched, drawing back, and Rob said hastily, "No, no, don't worry, I didn't do anything dangerous!" The flame in his palm flickered and extinguished as he grasped Matty's hand in his. It was warm and reassuring. "It seems an extremely unwise thing to do without knowing more."

Matty exhaled with relief. The gate had scared him. As had Lin, a little, if he was honest. What had scared him most was Arthur, though. Arthur had died because he had opened a gate in what Lin had called the shimmer. Matty remembered hearing the weight of it as he had spoken of it. The books here called it a border. It was clearly the same thing. If Rob opened the gate again, who knew what would happen? Matty was already poorly. He didn't want the same to happen to Rob.

Rob continued, "I wanted to see if I could follow Lin. Through the gate. To find out what's making you sick."

He said it as if it was nothing at all. A throwaway comment about popping down to the village to go to the post office.

Matty stared at him. "What?"

"Through the gate. I want to find Lin and see if he can help us. Help you." Rob's voice was no different from usual. A quiet, steady rumble as if he was suggesting something ordinary and safe. Not something supernatural and therefore incredibly dangerous.

"Through the gate?" Matty said, intelligently.

"Yes. It seems like it would be the best way to find out what's been happening. We haven't really got anywhere with Arthur's research." He gestured to the piles of books crowding the room around them. "This though... I've learned this."

Matty drew a steadying breath. "What else have you taught yourself? Do you think Arthur could do this?" The two questions came one after the other, spoken as soon as he thought them.

"Only one or two tricks. I can light a candle and put it out. And for some reason, the animals seem to come to me when I'm concentrating on doing things. That cross old tomcat that lives up in the barn has turned into my best friend since I started practising out there."

Matty thought. "Is that why the dogs were frantic the other night?"

The two farm collies were usually fairly stand-offish. As young dogs they had been welded to his father's side and once he'd died their loyalty had transferred to Arthur, but never in quite the same way. In the last few weeks they had started looking to Rob as they had looked to Dad. Matty had thought it was a natural transfer of affections now Arthur was gone, but perhaps there was more to it. He'd noticed them asking to go out a few evenings ago—they were only allowed into the house as far as the kitchen and much preferred to be out in the yard unless the weather was very bad—and when he'd demurred, they were absolutely insistent. They'd gone off silently but swiftly and half an hour later had accompanied Rob back inside with a great show of nonchalance.

A show of nonchalance that had almost equalled Rob's, thinking about it.

He looked at Rob closely. Rob's expression was sheepish. "What were you doing?" Matty asked. He used his firmest voice.

Rob looked down, his mouth twisting a little, ruefully. "I may have tried to make the gate appear." He hastily added, "Not to go through! Only to see if it was there!"

They had still been holding hands, absently, Matty still kneeling at his feet. Matty dropped Rob's warm, enfolding palm, stood, and crossed his arms, glaring down at him. "You just said you hadn't done anything dangerous!" Rob didn't lie. It was one of the things that Matty knew for certain about him.

Rob shot to his feet in turn and shoved his hands in his pockets, shoulders hunched defensively. "It *wasn't* dangerous! Really!" He walked over to the window, pacing uncomfortably, his hands in his pockets as he looked out through the uncovered panes to the dark night. "Sorry," he muttered, "I did try and make it appear." Matty waited. "I wanted to keep it from you, to keep you safe. I'm sorry, Matt." He turned back to face Matty. "I'd do almost anything to keep you safe." His mouth twisted a little with something like sadness or desperation around the words and Matty's heart twisted too, despite his anger. "If I can do this, and it's something that will make you safe, then I'll do it." He stepped a step toward Matty, shoulders still hunched, hands still in his pockets, looking at the floor. "I'm sorry I didn't tell you. I won't do that again."

Matty stepped closer across the threadbare Axminster carpet to meet him halfway. It was the least he could do. "Rob," he said softly. "Look at me?"

Rob met his eyes. They were as anguished in expression as his twisted mouth. Matty put his hands on his shoulders. "I'm not a fragile flower, love," he said. "And I'm not a stupid man." He squeezed through the soft wool of Rob's jumper. "I thought we were a team?" he said. "I want to be a team. I know you want to protect me. I want to protect you." He tightened and released his hands again, rubbing the curve of Rob's biceps.

"I don't know what I'd do if anything happened to you, now," Rob said, "I was ready for it in France. I knew there was a chance you might go west." He breathed out a harsh breath. "I've kind of got used to being back now and to us having a future after all. I don't want to lose you to this." He looked down, and then up again to meet Matty's eyes. He shut his eyes and Matty tightened his grip.

"No secrets though," Matty said. "If Arthur hadn't kept this a secret, he might still be alive. I don't want to lose you, either." He bit his lip and then smiled. "I've become used to having you about, you know."

Rob met his smile with one of his own. "Well. I suppose I'm handy with the cattle." He scuffed the toe of his slipper on the carpet.

"Yes. That's why. And the dogs like you. Goodness knows why, when you drag them off to magical doings in the barn." He stepped forward, closing the space between them and wrapping his arms around his lover. "Please, Rob. Don't keep secrets from me. Don't get yourself killed." He buried his face in the gap above Rob's collar, under his ear, where his neck was warm and smooth where he'd shaved earlier in the evening. Rob buried his face in the same place on Matty. They both smelled of Pears shaving soap. It satisfied something deeply primal in Matty that they shared a scent. In a slightly muffled voice, Matty added "You're too important to lose to this. To lose at all."

It was Rob's turn to push Matty back to arm's length. "You are too, Matty. You are too. It's tearing me up. Do you know you've started talking in your sleep?"

He didn't. He knew he'd been having dreams, though. He couldn't remember anything about them when he woke, merely a cloying sense of being trapped in something sticky, enveloped in mud or fog that sucked at him hungrily. He had been struggling with it for the last few weeks and often woke with the old soft sheets and blankets tangled round his legs in a sweaty mess. He thought he might have been dreaming about the trenches. "What do I say?" he asked.

Rob tugged him toward the wide red sofa and settled them both down on it, Rob lying on his back and Matty on his chest. They sometimes lay like this in front of the fire, drowsing in the dim light of an evening. It was comforting. Matty needed comfort.

"It's difficult to make out what you're saying," Rob said, once they were settled in their usual position. "Move your elbow. It's under my ribs." They shuffled themselves around. "That's better." He continued, "Sometimes you call for Arthur. Sometimes for me." He was breathing hard. "You call out that you're stuck and for us not to leave you." His arms tightened and relaxed again. "I won't leave you, Matty. I'm not leaving you."

He sounded as distressed as Matty felt when the nightmares woke him. Matty strove to change to subject. "Tell me about the shimmer," he asked. "Did you make the gate appear? What happened?"

"I could show you?" Rob said. "I've made it appear it a couple of times, out behind the byre where it started with Lin. And then a couple of times in the barn." He paused again. "I know it frightens you. It frightened me to start with, but there doesn't seem to be much to that part of it. Making it show up doesn't seem to be that difficult or need much energy drawn toward me to do it. I swear, I haven't tried to go through it." Matty flinched and Rob's surrounding arms tightened again. He nuzzled Matty's hair, where his head was tucked up under his chin. "Honestly, Matty..." Another pause. "I could show you in here, if you like. There isn't much to it."

Matty sat up, slowly, pushing himself off Rob's chest until he could get his legs under him. He perched astride Rob's thighs, looking down at him. Rob looked nervous. "Please believe me, Matty. Nothing happened. It was safe." Rob sat up himself, steadying himself with hands on Matty's hips and then sliding his arms up around Matty's back and drawing him close. Matty slid his arms round Rob too and Rob continued, "I feel like we're stuck now. We know a lot more from the books, I suppose, now we've managed to read through most of them. But it's not taking us any further forward practically. There's a chance that opening the gate might, and I want to do it." His jumper was soft and worn under Matty's cheek and his voice was as soft and enveloping despite the enormity of what he was saying.

They held each other for a moment more. Rob was steady, Matty reminded himself. He had always been steady. He didn't rush into things without thinking them through.

"Show me, then," Matty said, finally, drawing back and looking at him.

Rob wriggled his legs. "Let me sit up. I can't concentrate properly with you sat on my cock."

"I'm not sitting on your cock." Matty ground his hips down and round, in passing. "Oh. Perhaps I am." He grinned as he swung his leg over and stood to allow Rob to put his feet on the ground and sit in a more upright posture.

"How do we do it?" He wasn't sure at all about it, but Rob made good points. They knew a little more now, from the books. None of it was any good if they couldn't *use* it. And he really didn't want to end up like Arthur.

"Sit down here," Rob patted the sofa. "I need to be still and concentrate. I sort of tug at the world, in my head... Tug at the air? It's really hard to describe. It's like gathering threads or ribbons in my hands. Then I wait a moment for the energy to gather and pool. Then I can send it where I want." He looked at Matty. "It almost feels like wind. But not." He shook his head. "It sounds stupid, when I try and put it into words."

Matty put a hand on his arm reassuringly. "It doesn't at all. It just sounds like something you don't have the vocabulary for. It does make sense. To me, anyway." He squeezed Rob's arm before letting go again, withdrawing his hand and making a vague gesture. "Go on then. Show me?"

Rob nodded. "I don't know if I can talk whilst I do it. You stay there, then I know where you are. I can sort of feel you, once I start drawing the energy to me. I'm fairly certain I could suck energy from you if I wanted... I don't think that would be a good thing, somehow, what with all that's going on."

Matty nodded in agreement and drew his knees up onto the sofa and curled back against the armrest on the opposite end from Rob. "Can I talk to you?"

"I think it's better if it's quiet. So, I can concentrate. The cat jumped on my lap in the middle the second time I tried and scared me half to death."

Matty nodded again. "I'm ready, then."

Rob nodded back at him. "Right." He closed his eyes and leaned forward, elbows on his thighs. He took a few deep breaths, in through his nose and out through his mouth. Soft but deep, filling his lungs.

Matty watched him. There was a sense of calm growing around him, radiating out. Matty was right on the edge of it. It was like a soap bubble. Matty reached out a hand, decidedly tentatively, palm-first, toward it. He could feel the edge. He pressed, gently.

"Stop it!" Rob said in a low voice and Matty whipped his hand back into his lap as if burned.

"Sorry!" he said. "It's like a bubble."

"Yes. It feels like I'm sitting in the middle of it. When you touch it, I can feel it. It's distracting."

"Sorry," Matty said again. "I've stopped."

Rob opened his eyes briefly and shot him a smile. "I know, I can feel." Matty sensed the bubble contract a little, presumably as Rob moved his attention to talking. Rob closed his eyes again and it expanded back to where it had been. "I'm going to direct the energy toward the shimmer now," Rob said. "I don't know if you'll notice any change."

He lifted his right hand from his knee and stretched it out, much as he'd done when he showed Matty the pink flame. He pulled his ear nervously again before flexing his fingers, rather as if he were a piano maestro warming up before a performance.

A heat haze began to build about six feet in front of them, between the settee and the door to the red-tiled hall. Matty kept still. He could still feel the bubble of calm around Rob, but he was also aware that other things were happening. Rob was right, it was almost like a breeze, or the percussion blast from a shell. He couldn't tell where it was coming from or where it was going, but he was aware in a palpable but indescribable way that something unseen was moving around them.

As he watched, the heat haze became stronger. It expanded into an oval sheet about the height of a person and twice as wide. Rob made a satisfied sound and said, "There." When Matty looked at him, his eyes were open, and his palm was still extended. Rob stood and stepped toward it, arm still outstretched. He touched it with his fingers, and it rippled. "It buzzes," he said.

Matty sat with his arms wrapped round his knees. "Is that the gate itself? Are you pushing energy toward it?" he asked.

"Yes, a little. Once I start it, it seems to keep flowing until I cut it off. Like priming a pump." He swirled his fingers around in a circle and the haze followed them, like soap tracing. "I haven't done anything other than this. I'm not sure if it's the gate itself. Or if it's actually part of the shimmer. Do you want to feel it?"

Matty shook his head. "No. No, thank you. I... It feels wrong."

Rob nodded. "It doesn't feel *wrong* to me. Only different." He took another breath. "If I keep breathing into it, it expands, or it gets brighter. But not both at once. It's strange. It's not a gate, though, as it is. It's more like... a wall. Or maybe a door. I wondered if when it gets brighter, it's closer to opening."

"Do you think that's why they sometimes describe it as a border?" Matty asked.

"Perhaps. I don't know." Rob made a frustrated face. "That's the trouble, isn't it? We don't actually *know* anything. All these writings are by people who assumed that anyone reading *does* know things. Basic principles at least. I wish we knew where

Arthur had got the books from. And how long he'd been working with it." He poked sharply at the ripples with a frustrated index finger.

Suddenly, the place he poked began to glow and an ululating, screeching wail filled the room. The shimmer rippled alarmingly. Matty sprang to his feet, not sure whether to run forward or away. Rob looked equally taken aback. He withdrew his hand quickly, stepped back, and made a few swiping motions with his outstretched arm.

The shimmer shrank to a pinpoint and popped out of existence like Matty remembered it doing in the summer when Lin had used it as a gate. The wailing cry faded with it. The circle of calm that Matty could feel around Rob dissipated. He shivered and said, "That didn't happen before, did it?"

Rob turned to face him, having made sure the heat haze was gone. His face was pale and grim. "No. That didn't happen before."

MATTY UNFROZE AND WANDERED to the ornate oak sideboard a little unsteadily. That had been unsettling. He poured two measures of brandy into his mother's cut-crystal glasses and passed one to Rob, who looked as unnerved as he felt.

"That was the same sound that we heard before, wasn't it? The thing that Lin got you to throw the lamp at?"

"Yes, I think so." Rob knocked his brandy back in one gulp. Matty could see his hand shaking. He poured another measure into the glass Rob held out to him and Rob sipped at it. "It felt...sticky. It was trying to pull energy from me, in the same way I was pulling the energy to myself to make the shimmer appear." He sank back onto one of the armchairs.

Matty blinked and took a mouthful of his own drink, turning to rest his back against the sideboard. He tilted his head back against the top cupboards, the sharp edges of the carved relief on the doors digging reassuringly into the back of his scalp. The question came without thought. "Do you think that's what's draining me? That drained Arthur to death?" He took another drink and Rob matched his action, then put his glass down on the top of the sideboard and stepped close, drawing Matty into his arms. With the solid weight of the oak at his back and the enveloping warmth of Rob in front of him, Matty felt grounded, despite the other man's continued slight shaking.

"Bloody hell, Matty. What have we got ourselves into?" Rob said.

CHAPTER SIX: Marchant

Under the Outlands

There was a tug on the pulling line again. Marchant felt it even in his hazy, half-waking languor. It was tiny, but it was clear and sharp, a stinging thorn on the edge of his kias.

Not good.

He'd been trying to sever the connection for months now, completely ineffectually.

He sat up on the edge of the sleeping-ledge, feet firmly on the floor and elbows on his knees, hands shoved through his hair.

Break, damn you, he thought. *Just...break.* He visualised a knife, gleaming gold and edged with fire, and brought it down through the image of the pulling line he held in his mind, not-quite-visible to his everyday sight but completely visible and glowing in his kias-augmented vision.

The imaginary line bent under the imaginary knife, thinned, stretched...and sprang back into place like a rubber band.

It was no good. It was too strongly fixed.

He let go and gave a single, cut-off sob and stopped more sound emerging with a stifling gasp.

The small, stone-walled room was cool, warm enough under the blanket he'd been given, but now he was upright the drop in temperature had brought him to full waking. Waking was not a comfortable place to be. He'd lost count of the days, but he thought he'd been here going on for eighteen months. More than five hundred days, anyway.

"*God!*" The curse exploded out of him as his fingers tightened and pulled at his over-long hair with frustration, although his eyes were screwed shut. Why couldn't he cut the line? It shouldn't even still be there. The person he had the original connection with was dead. He'd felt him die. The line shouldn't still exist. It certainly shouldn't be connected to the dead man's brother.

He hadn't known what he was getting into when he'd originally started working with Arthur Webber, that was for sure. He rubbed his hands over his face and stood, taking the handful of steps across the flagged floor to the door leading to the small washroom and sanitary facilities. He poured a little water from the pitcher into the bowl and cupped his hands to splash it on his face and then dipped the flannel in, wringing it out, and putting it on the back of his neck. As usual, it was extremely cold and woke him entirely. He used the lavatory, still unable to work out how it didn't smell vile without a water flush or soil to sprinkle on top. Then he washed his hands with the small piece of soap he had left. He made a mental note to ask for some more.

It wasn't that they were keeping him in poor conditions. He had food, water, clean clothes, frequent if irregular exercise. But he was confined. He couldn't leave and go home. Plus, no-one would help him cut the line.

The living conditions were different to anywhere he'd ever stayed before. It was better than the Western Front and he supposed the poor bastards he'd left behind there would be grateful to exchange places with him if they were ever offered the opportunity. He'd be pleased to swap with them now, though. He'd had enough.

He'd been corresponding with Webber since he'd bumped into him in London a few weeks before the Coronation. So, nearly ten years. Literally bumped into him, in the hall of the Foreign Correspondent's Club in St James. Marchant had been walking as he read the paper—a terrible habit—and Webber had been doing the same thing but in the opposite direction down the carpeted hallway. They had collided head-on and then both stepped back in surprise, muttered an apology, and Marchant had been about to continue on his way when Webber had suddenly raised his head like a pointer taking scent. With his head cocked to one side in enquiry, he invited Marchant to take a drink with him in the library.

He'd presented Marchant with a utterly unfeasible tale of mysterious books and implausible magic that Marchant had rejected out of hand, and then—after glancing around cautiously to check whether they had company—conjured a small but perfectly formed violet flame in the palm of his hand. Marchant's rejection quickly turned into fascination and by the end of a week not only were they sleeping together but Marchant could produce his own burgundy-coloured flame.

After six months the sex had tailed off. But the magic became stronger as Marchant used it; and when Webber left London for his family farm, they'd continued to correspond and swap techniques. Occasional meetings for bed sport and trying new spells had meant that over the years they'd developed a visceral connection that Marchant could feel every time he brought the other man to mind.

Webber stayed at home when the war came, and Marchant took himself off to France with the Sunday Post. Their correspondence continued intermittently. Webber was getting more and more invested in a book he'd come across on his travels. Pulling energy from a 'border' that he said had infinite energy. Learning ever more complex spells. Marchant stopped being interested at that point. It sounded insane. Letters were difficult because of the censor, but Webber intimated that he was exploring a way to make a weapon that would end the war. The one time Marchant managed to visit him when he was back in England in 1916, he looked almost crazed, his previously immaculate grooming tattered around the edges, his hair wild, and his moustaches untrimmed. Marchant hadn't been able to get much sense out of him about his work with the energy.

After that, he'd felt the link between them becoming stronger and the energy becoming brighter, like an electric light running from a really good generator. If Marchant tried, he could take some of the energy to power his own minor excursions into spell-craft, making lights and suchlike...and he could feel when Webber drew Marchant's own energy back down the link to power whatever he was doing. Marchant wasn't that bothered by it. He had enough going on up to his armpits in mud and blood and bandages and trying to bang out copy that would simultaneously get past the censors and wasn't so bland that the paper would sack him. He started to feel that the war had been going on for ever and that the future stretched out in front of him as an interminable shattered land-scape of broken men and mechanised death.

One night in spring 1917, though, all that changed. He was in his bed at the Hotel St James when he felt Webber start to pull from him. Luckily, he was already lying down. The sensation got stronger and stronger and he began to feel sick and faint. Then abruptly, the sensation became painful, a sharp, spiking pain in his abdomen. He couldn't bear it any longer and he *tugged* back. Like he would on a rope if the man tied in front was going too fast. Instead of easing off though, Webber continued to pull, harder and harder.

Marchant found himself on the floor, gasping with pain, barely coherent. Eventually he gathered himself and began to pull back more firmly, taking back what was his. An observer would have had no idea what was taking place—an unseen battle for dominance on the etheric plane. Marchant got a small advantage when Webber faltered for some reason and he continued to pull. To pull and pull and pull. Webber was much stronger than Marchant remembered. The energy seemed unending, flowing bright and strong into his body. He found himself feeling sick and faint and overwhelmed for the opposite reason than he had before...it was simply *too much*. Too much. He had to get rid of it. So, he *pushed* and *twisted* and started to push the energy out of himself as well as accepting the flow from Webber. It was now flowing into him on its own, he wasn't having to pull at all.

He realised he was pushing the energy into the mythical border Webber had spoken of when a sheet of something like heat haze slowly appeared and started to glow. He lay on the floor unable to move and watched the shimmering haze grow from a small, almost invisible patch to a circle the size of a church doorway. As his struggle to contain the energy flowing into him from Webber continued, as the power flowed through him and out again, the patch grew brighter and brighter and brighter. Webber started to pull back from him and Marchant fought it. He wasn't going to let Webber drain him like that again. He pulled and tugged sharply, and physically rolled away from Webber's pull, toward the light.

There was a clattering bang like a shell going off and an animal screaming. It wasn't him making that high-pitched noise, but he was certainly shouting. He'd rolled right into the border, into the light. It hurt. God, it hurt. He'd never felt anything like it. The pain went all the way down to his marrow and he rolled over onto all fours on the carpet and started retching.

It took him a while to realise he wasn't kneeling on the carpet at all. He was on sandy, gritty ground, dry except for the bile soaking in where he had vomited. The animal screaming was still there, but he was returning to himself and had stopped making noise. There were other people shouting. He seemed to be the centre of a circle of people, all milling about him. The extra power flooding into him had stopped, although he could still feel Webber at the end of the line.

Someone said something in a liquid language he didn't understand and a pair of hands under his armpits pulled him to his feet. They weren't particularly gentle getting him up, but when he started retching again, they eased him down carefully. He didn't pay much attention to what was going on around him until he'd finished retching again and lay stretched out on the dry sand.

By then, the shouting around him had quietened a little, although there were still a lot of legs he could see through his half-closed eyelids. He didn't open his eyes any further, taking the time to gather himself. The feet he could see were mostly clad in low, comfortable looking boots with trousers that tucked into them. There were no uniform boots or puttees that he could see. The colours of the clothes were muted browns and greens and blues. No skirts.

At that point, someone poked him with the toe of one of the boots and said something in that lilting language. He flinched before he could stop himself and whoever it was crouched beside him and put a hand on his shoulder to push him backward. The hovering nausea and dizziness returned as he propped himself up on his elbows and opened his eyes properly.

He was in the centre of a ring of faces staring down at him.

The person crouching beside him said something to him in that music-like tongue he didn't understand and then stopped and looked at him for a moment. Marchant felt a slight touch on his energy field and then, after a pause, the man said slowly, in English, "Who are you? What are doing here?"

Marchant dragged the sleeve of his pyjamas roughly across his mouth, trying to get rid of the disgusting taste of vomit. "Peter Marchant. I'm Peter Marchant. And I don't know what I'm doing here." He scrambled to his feet, followed by his questioner, and the circle around him opened out slightly as the watchers took a step back.

The animal he had heard screaming screamed again, further away this time. A couple of the men in the crowd turned to look in the direction it came from and one said something to the other before they looked at him again. He felt a sharp tug to his centre, where he could still feel the connection to Webber.

"What's going on?" he asked. "Who are you? Where is this? What happened?"

The person who had been crouching beside him looked to an older woman who was at the front of the crowd. "Malach?" he said. She stepped forward.

"You are in the undercaves of the Frem," she said.

THAT HAD BEEN EIGHTEEN months ago.

He had been treated with courtesy, but it was clear to him that the Frem, whoever they were, were keeping him prisoner. He had done his best to learn that bell-toned, liquid language of theirs, despite everyone he spoke to being able to speak to him in English. He had asked about it, early on, and Lin, who he had most contact with, had looked him with a raised eyebrow and said, "It is in your kias. Anyone can touch your kias and the words become clear to us. Is it not so with your people?"

Marchant had shaken his head. "No. And kias...you mean the magic? The energy?"

Lin nodded.

"I only know of one other person who even knows it exists and he is on the other end of this line that I can't break. And tried to drain me."

Lin nodded again. "It is an extraordinarily bad thing, the line. No good things ever come of a permanent connection.

Severing it is almost impossible now it has been used for such strong work. We cannot break it safely for you without him here and we only cross to the Delfland in dire crisis."

Marchant took from this that his situation was not a dire crisis. "What happens to me, then?" he had asked Lin. "What do I do?"

Lin looked at him almost sympathetically. "You wait." He stopped walking and turned to face Marchant. They were walking their regular circle around some of the inner halls where there seemed to be a market and places that sold food. It was crowded and humid and warm. "You wait, and because his kias is bleeding through you and into the shimmer, eventually he will die, and the line will die with him." He was very matter of fact.

Marchant swallowed. "He'll die?"

"Yes. His kias will eventually run out." Lin looked at him sternly. "This is why using kias is not a game, as you have been using it. And Webber." He paused. "Well. From what you say, about the books and 'magic spells', Webber seems to have been using not only his own kias but pulling from the shimmer on a regular basis. And of course, from you. Without your consent." He looked angry. "This is not done. It is dangerous. As you have found out."

Marchant swallowed. "I didn't know."

"No. And that is why you are still alive." He looked at his feet, drew a pattern in the dirt ground with his toe, and then scuffed it out again before looking up at Marchant again. "Malach is fair. It is the job of the Ternants to protect the shimmer. If too much is drawn from it, the barrier between the worlds becomes thin. Things can cross. Carnas." He bit his lip and dropped his eyes again. "You heard one, I think, when you first arrived. You do not want them in your world." He swallowed. "They are bad enough here."

"Carnas?" Marchant repeated.

"Yes. Carnas. They feed on kias. They drain it when they can. They are drawn to the shimmer, but they cannot pull energy from it. They can only draw from people. Your people and my people. I know not why. But they are dangerous. Sometimes the Ternants use them to protect the shimmer...the Ternants are charged with keeping the shimmer safe from harm. They monitor it. They are immensely powerful.

"So, they could tell when Arthur... When Webber—" He wasn't going to think of him as Arthur anymore, "—when Webber tried to pull all the kias from me and I pulled it back and it went into the shimmer?"

"Yes. The carnas sense that kind of manipulation of kias. As do some of the Ternants. Some of them are exceptionally old and skilled. That's why they were there when you breached the shimmer. And you heard the carnas calling. They brought it with them." He turned to start walking again. "If it had been one of our people who had done what you had done, then they would have let the carnas have you. You were lucky."

Marchant swallowed. "Let the carnas have me?"

"Yes." Lin swallowed too. "They like to maul their prey as they drain them. They usually bite out the throat as they feed."

Marchant was silent and after a few moments, Lin continued. "What you did, when Webber tried to use your kias for whatever he was doing, reversed the way the line works. You permanently changed it by the strength of your response. He had taken so much kias from the shimmer when he started working that he was incandescent with it. You took all that from him in the course of defending yourself. Kias is now trickling constantly from him to you and from you into the shimmer, because you opened another line to it to get rid of all the kias. Your system couldn't hold it."

Marchant nodded. "I can feel it. But whatever I do, I can't shut it off."

Lin nodded too. "Yes. I can see it. It was created with such force, you were in such a panic, that there is nothing that can be done without Webber here."

"Why can't I go back and fix it from there?"

Lin shook his head. "They...we...don't trust you. You were using kias that you did not understand. You created a gate in the shimmer. I have never heard of one person doing that by themselves. Even the Ternants work together when they send hunters through. I think it scared them. You and Webber scared them. They aren't sure of your purpose. With you here and Webber there, you cannot work together again."

Marchant nodded glumly. He could see their point. "I wasn't doing anything. But Webber told me he was creating a weapon to stop the war."

"A weapon of kias strong enough to stop a war without doing catastrophic damage to the shimmer is extremely unlikely. If he has created one or thinks he has, then there is even more reason not to send you home to support him. And now...with his kias draining into you and thence into the shimmer...you can see how Malach wishes you to stay here until he is no longer a problem."

Marchant could see. He didn't like it, but he could see.

He spent his time learning the language, Fremish, and getting Lin to teach him how to use his kias properly. In return Lin picked his brains about life in the Delfland. He was never allowed anywhere unescorted and Lin wasn't allowed to take him outside the undercaves. He understood the Frem lived largely underground. Outside their caves was the Outland. The Outland was mostly desert as far as he understood it. Very hot or very cold. There were plants and animals, including the carnas, that were adapted for the environment, but it was more comfortable for the Frem to reside deep in the mountains. Some of them never went outside at all. The young people slept in barrack-like dormitories and family groups had sets of rooms together. Almost every adult was part of a family group of some kind or another as far as he could make out. It wasn't clear if they married in a traditional sense and Marchant wasn't going to ask. Lin mentioned that he was in the dormitories and had no family yet and he left it at that.

The Outlands were on the edge of the Inner Hills and the Inner Hills were not somewhere the Frem went. There was some sort of battle for territory over the Inner Lands that they had exempted themselves from by moving to the Outlands and taking on oversight of the shimmer. That was all that Marchant was able to make out. It seemed unnecessarily complicated, but he supposed that if he tried to explain Imperial politics to Lin, Lin would be equally at a loss.

One day, the kias coming to him from Webber became so faint that he thought it was gone. He hammered on the door of his room furiously, shouting for Lin. Lin came and looked at him with eyes half shut and then said, "I'm going to get Malach," and disappeared. He returned a few moments later with Malach and another person Marchant recognised as one of the Ternants.

"It's fading," he said, in a panicked voice. "What do I do?" There had been some suggestion that if the line to the shimmer was not closed off at the same time as the line draining Webber, Marchant's own kias would start to drain into the shimmer in the same way.

"Sit," Malach ordered. Marchant sat on the bed, abruptly.

The three of them hovered over him in a semicircle with Malach in the centre. She withdrew a green stone on a leather thong from the folds of cloth around her neck and held it in the palm of her hand. "Now, please," she said. The other two were silent with half-closed eyes and Marchant was aware of kias flowing from them to her. "Be still, Marchant," Malach ordered him. "We will try and sort this out once and for all."

There was a period of kias shifting and swirling around him that he didn't really follow, and he was aware of his link to Arthur...Webber he had trained himself to call him now...fading and becoming more and more faint. It paused. Then it stopped. The link draining into the shimmer stopped at the same time and Malach made some sort of tying off gesture that seemed to bind everything together.

He sighed in relief. It was over. He could go home.

Then he realised that far from stopping, the flow of kias had resumed more strongly, and his link to the shimmer had re-opened. He looked at Malach. "What's happening?"

She lowered the stone, clutched in her hand. "He has passed his end of the line on to someone else. I think, a family member." She shut her eyes again and grasped at the stone. Lin and the third woman were silent as she sorted out what she could feel. "Yes. The first man is gone. The one with the strong kias, who stole from you and from the shimmer. But he has tied the line to a sibling."

She opened her eyes and looked at him. "I am sorry, Marchant. His death should have been an end to it. I don't know how he has done it, but the line now links you to the new person. I cannot untie you without causing you harm." Her eyes were grey, sympathetic, but unbending. "If the other person's kias keeps flowing to you and you don't have that out line, it will hurt you, so although I could tie that, it would be wrong to do so." She tucked the stone back in the neckline of her loose clothing matter-of-factly. "We must go on as before. This one has no knowledge of kias or pulling. It won't take long and then you will be free and can return to your Delfland."

"What do you mean 'it won't take long?'" Marchant stood up, toe to toe with her and she stepped back to give him room.

"Eventually his kias will drain through you into the shimmer and he will die. Then you will be free."

Marchant looked at her. "He'll die?"

"Yes. As his kias drains. Was I not clear?" She was annoyed with him.

"You were clear. I just don't like it. I remember Webber's brother. Matthew. He doesn't deserve to die because Arthur and I were playing with things we didn't understand."

She looked at him. "If he doesn't use kias the drain will be very small. He will live a long time." She turned and swept out, her companion following her.

Lin lingered, shutting the heavy door behind them in the stone archway, and sat on the bed next to Marchant as Marchant sank down again. He put his elbows on his knees and his head in his hands. "I am sorry, Marchant. Peter." He put his hand on Marchant's back tentatively. "I did not know this was a thing that could happen. I am sorry."

Marchant let himself take a tiny bit of comfort from the hand between his shoulder blades. It was an exceedingly long time since he'd been touched by anyone.

"What happens now?" he asked.

"We wait, I suppose. Unless you can cut this line yourself?"

Marchant visualised giving it an experimental tweak. Nothing happened except a flex and swell of kias toward him. If he messed with it too much, he was going to end up draining the poor kid quicker than was already happening. He shook his head. "No. I can't."

"Then we wait."

HE EXISTED FOR A COUPLE of months on a day to day basis, staying in his cell, meditating to learn to control his kias, trying to cut the line draining into him from Webber's brother and the line draining out of him into the shimmer, and failing at both those things. The people he met on his supervised per-ambulations and trips to the baths were kind, polite, smiling. And purposefully distant. He wasn't really lonely, because he had never been a lonely person. If he had been though, he would have been desolate. The only person who talked to him about anything in depth was Lin. And Lin wasn't always there. He didn't say where he went, except for 'Malach is sending me out' and Marchant didn't ask.

He was aware of small changes in the energy coming through him. Matty was learning to use kias. Maybe not even consciously using it, but whatever he was doing was making the link between them stronger. He wasn't drawing energy from Marchant—Marchant didn't know if that was even possible—so he must be drawing from the shimmer itself, using it and then letting it flow on to Marchant and thus through him, back to the shimmer. That wasn't good, but Marchant had no way of warning him.

Lin had a few days away at one point and came back dishevelled and grim looking. It had coincided with an enormous swell in energy from Matty and a push-pull coming down the line.

"What did you do?" Marchant asked him, the minute he stepped into the cell. "Where did you go? I *felt* it, Lin! You did something to Matty!"

Lin was silent for a moment, then let out a breath as if he'd made a decision.

"Not deliberately," he said. "There was a weakness discovered in the shimmer." He shook his head as Marchant opened his mouth to speak. "I don't know why." He stepped toward the bed and collapsed to sit on Marchant's neatly tucked blankets. "A carnas nearly managed to break through. They sent me to stop it." He put his head in his hands. "There's something going on, Peter. I don't know what. I don't know why they are keeping you here. It's not altruism. There must be a reason. I don't understand what's happening."

It was Marchant's turn to put his hand on Lin's back. "I don't understand at all, Lin. I didn't think it was possible for the line to transfer to Arthur's brother. And if he's not using kias, how can there be a weakness in the shimmer?"

"Webber transferred the line to his brother. That much I know. There's no other way for that to have happened. Whether it was intentional is impossible to say without speaking to the man. And I didn't have a chance, not properly."

"But you did see him? How is he?"

"As far as I could see he was healthy. There was another man with him there, who seemed to know a little about the gate and the shimmer. I didn't have much time with them. But they looked well enough." He rubbed his hands over his face and looked up at Marchant. "I closed the gate. I don't know who was trying to open it, or what was going on. There was a carnas. Someone must have tried to send a carnas through and that would have been terrible for your people." He drew his hair back from his face with his fingers and sighed. "I need to sleep. I came as soon as I could; I knew you'd have felt it." Marchant realised that Lin's shoulders were wet. He must have come the moment he'd got back.

"Go and sleep," he said. "We'll talk about it later. It's not like I'm going anywhere."

CHAPTER SEVEN: Cutting the Line

As the year turned down toward Christmas, Rob practised and practiced with his kias. He was determined. It was obvious to anyone who knew him that Matty wasn't well. He looked peaked and he was exhausted at the end of a day's work. If the screaming thing they had heard twice now was the cause of the illness, had its claws into him as both Arthur and the mysterious writer of the book had described, then Rob was going to catch it and he was going to make it stop. Whatever that took.

He kept what he was doing hidden from Matty as much as he could. He didn't want to worry him. It wasn't exactly that he kept it a secret, more that he chose times when Matty wasn't around. If Matty asked what he'd been up to, Rob told him. If Matty came upon him working, he didn't stop. But he didn't seek Matty out to tell him what he was doing.

Matty didn't ask questions really, either. The weather was dull and rather mild for the time of year and it was nice not to have to break ice on the water for the animals every single morning. It gave them more time for other things. Matty seemed to have given up his almost frenzied search to find out what ailed him now they had decided it was the carnas. He was quiet and resigned in a way that hurt Rob's heart to watch.

Rob gathered his courage and brought it up one day during the week before Christmas, when they had been reminiscing about holiday seasons past.

"Arthur was giddy about Christmas," Matty said, with an affectionate smile. "Before he went away, anyway. One year he smeared marmalade all over the church door handle and people were licking it off themselves all through the service." He chuckled. "Father thrashed the life out of him when we got home, but I overheard him tell Mother later that it was the funniest thing he'd seen for years. Squire Elmhurst had it all over his gloves."

"That was before my time," Rob said. "I don't remember that. I remember the year your Mama put too much brandy on the pudding and it nearly set the kitchen alight, though."

Matty laughed. "Yes! That was the year she caught Arthur kissing Emily Beelock under the mistletoe before church. She was so put out. I'm not sure which of them she scolded more."

There was a warm, intimate silence.

"I miss them," Matty said.

"I do too," Rob answered, staring into his cup of tea. They were sat at the kitchen table, putting off washing the supper things. "I never really had a family until I came here. Dad did his best, but we travelled around quite a bit before he settled us here and I never met his family, or Mother's."

"Do you remember her?" Matty asked.

"No, not really. She died when I was two or three, I think. I should have had a baby brother, Father always said. Then of course he went when I was at the end of school. I was lucky your parents were so kind. They could have simply sent me on my way. But they took me on instead and here we are."

"They always looked on you as a member of the family," Matty said. "Father always said taking your Dad on was the best thing he ever did for the cattle. He was the finest cowman he ever had, he said."

"He was good with the livestock," Rob said. "He always worked with animals, wherever we were. People would ask him for help before they called the veterinary."

"Yes, I remember Elmhurst asking him to look at that pony one year. He was very impressed. Father was worried the squire would try and coy him away."

"I don't think he'd have gone," Rob said. "He'd found his place here, same as I did." He looked up at Matty. "It feels like it, anyway. 'Specially now."

Matty smiled at him over the scrubbed oak table. "It feels like it to me, too."

That gave Rob an opening.

"I don't want to lose this, Matty. I don't want to lose you." He paused. "I've been practising controlling my kias. I want to try and go through the door and find Lin. See if he can help us."

Matty blinked at him and bit his lip. "It's dangerous," he said after a moment. "It's probably more dangerous than just hoping it goes away."

Rob pulled his ear uncomfortably. "Yes. It probably is. But it's worth it. For me, it's worth it." He coughed. That was more than enough about his emotions. Focus on the practical things.

"I think that if we went out beyond the barn, where the gate opened before, and tried it there, there would be enough room. And it would keep everything away from that house."

"Is that where you've been practising?" Matty's voice was steady and Rob answered in kind.

"Yes. It seemed like it was sensible to keep it away from the house as much as possible."

"So, you do admit that it's dangerous?" Matty's steady voice had an edge.

"Of course it's dangerous, Matt. Of course it is! But I can't think of any other way to help you."

"What about..." Matty was cautious, obviously thinking it out as he went, "What about... if this connection is real and I'm attached to something or something is attached to me... what about trying to break it off? Before we do this?" He bit his lip and looked firmly at Rob. "Because whatever you do, you're not doing it alone, Rob. If you go through the gate, I'm going with you." He paused. "So, let's try this first?"

Rob pondered. It made sense. If there was some sort of link between Matty and the carnas and that was what was making him ill, then getting its claws out of him would be a good thing. He wasn't sure how. But it surely couldn't hurt to try?

"We could try it," he said, cautiously. "I don't know how, though. We'll have to have another look through the green book. Maybe there's something in there?"

"Perhaps," Matty said. "There was something, I think. It was in Latin, though. Damned old."

Rob ran his hand through his hair. "Can you remember where in the book it was?"

"I'm not sure exactly, but it won't take long to leaf through it. Or do you want to go to bed and do it tomorrow?"

"Bed sounds good." Rob leered at Matty in a friendly fashion. "Let's look it up tomorrow."

ALTHOUGH IT WAS A TUESDAY, it was the day before Christmas Eve and Mrs Beelock had got her son to take her into Taunton in the pony cart to do a bit of shopping and wouldn't be back until late, so they had the place to themselves to continue their faint line of research. There wasn't much. But it was something. Bound between larger pages of the book, a fragment in faded brown ink that Matty had translated from the Latin:

Gather your power
See your target as a fish on a line
Pull sharply
Like a fish on a line you may have to fight it
Play out the line as with a fish in the river
Power splashing like sunlit water
Until held steady,
You can grasp your target with your hands
And strike to exsanguinate.

It sounded simple. Everything sounded simple in the green book and the simpler it sounded, the more layers there were underneath it to trip you up. It wasn't a beginner's instruction manual. It was a collection of notes made by people who knew what they were doing, or who thought they did. Rob loathed them all on principle.

The carnas sounded extremely intimidating. The little about them in either book, the green or the brown, did not lead Rob to think they would be easy to kill. Assuming that was what the direct translation of the Latin *exsanguinate* meant. It might only mean cut enough to make it bleed. They were dependent on instructions written down by someone a long time ago who may or may not have got the wrong end of the stick. Or been completely off their chump. Rob still wasn't convinced he was off his own, if he was perfectly honest.

"So what?" Matty asked, somewhat fractiously. "You do this fishing thing and then I hit it with the wood axe?"

"More or less," Rob said, trying to sound as if he knew what he was doing. "Although I was thinking that shooting at it might be better. First, anyway."

Matty swallowed. "All right," he said. He paused. "It's not a great plan, Rob."

"Well, no. But it's the only one I've got at this point. Surely, it's worth trying, Matty? I'll practice first. I'm getting passably good with working with the power. If I concentrate, I can see that there's a silver thread coming off you, going somewhere else."

Matty looked alarmed. "Don't touch it!" he said. "Don't do anything with it until we're ready. We don't want that thing coming through here until we're ready for it!"

"I just want it done with!" Rob replied testily. "I want you safe, Matty. This is all wrong and I wish I knew more about it and could fix it easily. But I can't. This is the best I can do!"

Matty looked cross as well as alarmed.

Rob never raised his voice in anger. Ever. He swallowed and tried to calm down. "I'm sorry, I'm sorry," he said, hands flat on the kitchen table where they'd spread the books out to be warm without having to bother with lighting the sitting room fire. "I've stopped. I've stopped shouting."

Matty's face relaxed a bit. "It's fine," he said, clearly trying to mean it. "I'm scared, though."

"Yes, me too. I don't like things I don't understand properly. This is a whole load of things I don't understand. It's making me cranky."

"Do you want to have a try now? Just to get it over with?"

"We could?" Rob wasn't confident he could do it. And he wasn't confident they'd be able to do the exsanguination part if he could do the pulling part. The carnas seemed pretty tough creatures. But having a go seemed better than waiting for Matty to get weaker and weaker whilst they messed about never being quite ready to try.

"I'll get the shotgun loaded." Matty was grim. "I've got Father's as well. If I load both, that's four shots."

Rob felt his face heat. "Er. I have a Luger out in the barn, locked in the bottom of the poison cupboard. So that's another eight. I've only got the one cartridge."

Matty looked at him with raised eyebrows. "All right, then. Good to know." He said it with some asperity.

Rob stood up and picked up the breakfast plates. "It seemed like a good idea the time, all right? I wasn't exactly in a good frame of mind when they shipped me home. I thought having a pistol might be useful in the future." He clattered the crockery into the sink. "Which it looks like might," he added under his breath. Then, to Matt again, "I took it off a chap we captured, near the end. They were weren't going to let me keep my own, were they?"

Matty came up behind him and slid his arms around his waist as Rob looked down at his own hands in the soapy dishwater. Neither of them had their jackets on yet and it was nice to feel the warmth of his lover pressed down his back, chin on his shoulder, without the barrier of buttons and anything thicker than their woollen pullovers.

"Sorry," Matty said, eventually, arms tightening slightly as he spoke. "That was unnecessary."

Rob shook his head mutely. "It wasn't. What do I need a pistol for, out here? The war's over. It's not coming back. We're safe."

Matty was silent for a bit longer. "Well, we're not, really, are we? Not with all this going on. Whatever it is. So, it's a good job you did bring it back. Let me get the shotguns and then we can go over to the barn and get it. Do you want to do this inside? It's raining again."

THEY SET UP IN THE barn. They dragged one of the battered deal chairs from the table in the old farmhands' sitting room at the stove's end out into the partitioned-off stable area they kept for handling the bull. It was the most secure area they could think of to contain the carnas if things got out of hand and Rob thought he'd be better able to concentrate sitting down.

Matty loaded the long shotguns with the ease of practice and leaned them against the wall. He cleaned them regularly and they used them for rabbits and suchlike for the pot. Since he'd come home from the army, his distaste for guns was always clear to anyone who knew him. Rob broke the Luger and checked it was working smoothly before loading the cartridge of eight bullets and putting one in the chamber. He'd been maintaining it out of habit, more or less, and it was in good condition.

He passed it to Matty, grip first. Their hands met as Matty took it and neither of them let go. "Shoot first, Matty. Don't give it a chance," Rob said.

Matty nodded. "Yes. I will," he said, drawing it gently toward him. "Don't worry about this part of it. I can do this part. You concentrate on your bit."

Rob reluctantly let go of the muzzle of the pistol. "Let's start then," he said, turning his back on Matty and needlessly arranging the chair.

"When you're ready." Matty leaned against the wall beside the chair, between it and the heavy stable door. His job was to open it and haul Rob out if things went badly.

Rob sat in the chair. It was flush with the heavy partition and he took a moment to centre himself and feel the solid wall at his back. Matty was another reassurance at his side. "I'm going to shut my eyes to start with, at least," Rob told him. "I can concentrate better."

"Go on then," Matty said. "I'm going to put a hand on your shoulder though, if that won't put you off?"

"It'll probably help. I've got to pick up the feel of the thread coming from you before I can pull on it."

Matty put his hand on his shoulder and even through his thick winter coat it was a warm, comforting presence. Rob wondered how much of what he could feel was physical-Matty and how much was kias-Matty. It didn't really matter; he was happy the other man was there.

He was putting it off.

He took a breath and shut his eyes as he did so, focusing on his energy field. As he breathed in, he breathed in kias. As he breathed out, he released the kias he had gathered into his own system, imagining it as a rubber balloon with him at the centre, expanding as the kias filled it. It wasn't hard. He'd done this before. Matty's hand rested firmly, immutable, connecting them together.

When he opened his eyes, he could see Matty's energy field as a faint, glowing cloud of kias around him. The silver thread that was leeching his kias led away from him, off to where Rob could faintly sense the shimmer without actually being able to see it and thence to who knew where. As the book instructed, Rob visualised an imaginary hand, reaching for it and pulling it toward him. He'd never really liked fishing and he certainly wasn't going to take it up as a hobby after this, he thought, grimly.

It was surprisingly hard to do.

The thread felt...sticky. Not like a fibre thread at all. And not like a hosepipe, which was the other thing he'd thought about. He gave it a tentative mental tug and it flexed a little, like a live thing might under his hands.

He tried very hard not to think of it as alive and gave it another, stronger pull. It bent toward him and then flexed back into place. Hell. Matty's fingers squeezed and released on his shoulder.

"All right?" Matty asked.

"Yes. You?" He couldn't spare much concentration for speech.

"It felt odd for a moment. As if someone was pulling my hair. Except it was pulling at my stomach."

"I'm going to do it again. Hold fast." He pulled as hard and as fast as he could and felt a definite give at the other end of the thread. Quickly, before he could lose his nerve, he visualised himself pulling hand over hand, as if he was hauling on a rope, reeling whatever it was anchored to back toward him.

Eventually he had to pause and bring in more kias to himself, let it build again. It was hard to keep hold of the thread he'd spooled closer and breathe the kias in and out whilst he did that, and the thing at the other end must have realised his attention was divided and tried harder to pull away.

"No, you don't!" he said, angrily, and started tugging again.

Matty's breathing beside him was strained. "I'm fine," he said, before Rob could ask. "Keep going."

"Don't know if I can," Rob replied and Matty answered him with another squeeze of his shoulder.

He took a deep breath and began to pull again with his mind. Over and over and over, visualising coiling the thread at his feet as he would have on a ship's deck. Whatever he was pulling was becoming harder and harder to drag toward them and eventually Rob ground to a halt again. The sweat was dripping off him despite the coldness of the December barn and his breathing was laboured.

"And again," Matty said. "I can feel it, Rob. You're doing it. It's...shaking? Trembling? I don't know. Keep going." He raised the Luger in his right hand, his left still reassuringly firm on Rob's shoulder.

Rob took another three deep, gathering breaths and threw all his kias forward, tugging with desperation on the cord. The carnas resisted. It didn't move at all. Then slowly, slowly, inch by terrible inch, Rob felt it sliding forward toward them.

"It's coming!" he ground roughly. "Get ready. Shoot it!"

With all his remaining strength of all kinds, he gave a great, tumultuous, enormous pull. Suddenly he could see the shimmer. It was a wall of pale light flickering across the middle of the stable. There was a brighter gate set in it. He tugged again and the gate bulged and roiled. A final time...and here it was. Whatever was at the end of the thread burst through the gate.

The effort put Rob on the floor, breath almost barking in and out of his chest, mental grip on the cord as firm as he could make it so the thing couldn't get away. He was aware of the shimmer flickering and dying behind him as he rolled, and he pulled at the thread with what he had left of his strength to steady it for Matty to shoot the thing.

Only as he rolled over to look, instead of the screaming carnas they were expecting, it was a man.

CHAPTER EIGHT: An Unexpected Arrival

"Shoot it! Shoot!" Rob was yelling from beside him on the floor, flailing.

The man lay on a few feet away, groaning, curled in a ball, arms protecting his head.

Matty had been expecting a carnas or some other twisted creature, not a human. It foxed him momentarily. Then, "It's a person!" he shouted back at Rob. "Grab him!"

They both piled forward onto the new arrival and there was a cartoonish mess of arms and legs and swearing which gradually slowed to three people in a heap panting heavily, which was a lot less traumatic than he had expected when they started.

One of them was being sick. It was the man who had come through the shimmer, who was at the bottom of the pile. Matty hastily rolled to one side, out of the way.

Their prisoner did nothing to escape but continued to retch.

Rob rolled aside and sat propped against the wood of the barn wall; head tilted back. He looked as if he might be sick too. Matty clambered to his feet and stood against the wall beside him with the Luger held loosely by his side, ready for any trouble.

He could still feel the *thing* pulling at his stomach, each time the man retched. It was horrible. As if something was pulsing to get out.

The man struggled to his hands and knees and continued to hack up nothing very much. As soon as he was able to speak, he ground out, "Cut it! Cut the line!"

Rob's head jerked forward like a terrier catching the scent of a rat.

"What?" he said. "What did he say?"

"Cut the line?" Matty said.

"Cut the line!" the man repeated. "Cut it if you can, for God's sake!" He was still on his hands and knees and Rob shuffled forward to kneel beside him, hand on his back.

"How do I cut it?" he asked. "Tell me and I'll do it!"

"You have to use your kias." He spun away from Rob, over on to his back, arm shielding his eyes. "God, it's bright in here. Cut it with your kias. They didn't tell me how. But do it. The Webber boy will die if you don't."

Rob blanched where he was sitting on his heels in the middle of the stable.

He looked at Matty and his eyes were dark holes of misery. "I can try a cut," he said. "Perhaps that'll work."

He drew his pocket-knife. The book had said *strike to exsanguinate*, Matty thought. The implication was that a simple cut would not work. "Use your kias too," he said, echoing the stranger. "Perhaps if you use kias too then it'll work without full exsanguination."

"They didn't think it would," the man said, unprompted and misinterpreting slightly. "The Ternants said if they cut it without him there, we'd both die. And if we don't cut it, he'd die anyway. We need to be in the same place for it to have a chance of working, and it's the only chance. You need to cut it. I don't care if it kills me. I'm past caring." He took his arm down from over his face and Matty saw he was familiar.

"Marchant?" he said. Arthur's friend. A journalist. Bloody hell. That was a turn up for the books.

"Yes." His voice was rough. He was still breathing heavily. "Hello, Webber." He coughed. "I'm sorry about your brother. This is probably his fault, though."

Matty stared at him.

"Do what you need to do to cut it," Marchant said. "I'm ready. I've had enough. I'm ready. Please? I'm begging you." He looked from Matty to Rob. "You're Curland, aren't you? I remember you from when I visited Arthur. Do it. Please. At least one of us should be free of it and I'm ready. Please."

Rob looked at Matty again. Matty nodded, giving absolution. "Try it," he said. He looked at Marchant, who had his arm back over his eyes. "He's going to cut your palm, Marchant," he said. "Hold still."

Marchant nodded. Matty could see he was biting his lip in anticipation.

Rob took hold of the arm Marchant hadn't thrown over his eyes and pressed it down to the packed earth of the barn, paused, turned the arm so the hand was palm up, and then put his knee on the forearm. Marchant winced. Rob fumbled his pocket-knife out of his pocket and eased the blade free.

"Steady now," he said, as if he was gentling an animal.

"Just do it," Marchant said.

Holding the arm steady with his knee and his left hand pressed down on the fingers, Rob took a breath in and shut his eyes. Matty assumed he was gathering his kias. A second later, he struck with the blade, quickly and decisively, slashing a great gash open across Marchant's palm.

Marchant flinched but didn't make a sound.

The stable was filled with nothing but the sound of men breathing as they both watched the blood pool on the floor under him. He still had his other arm flung over his eyes as he opened and shut his palm a few times.

"It's not working," he said. "I can still feel it."

Matty could feel it too. The thing in his stomach was twisting and furling and turning. In fact, as he observed the sensation, he began to feel dizzy.

Marchant suddenly sat up and pushed Rob off him. "Get off me," he said. "I'm not going anywhere." Rob fell back and Marchant knelt up, cradling his dripping hand against his chest. He looked at Matty.

"It's not working. I can feel it still draining into me from you. You've gone green." He pushed at Rob. "Get him sat, he's going to faint."

Matty did feel nauseated. He staggered as Rob guided him to sit on the floor and put his head between his knees.

"It's not enough," Marchant said. "You're going to have to cut my throat."

He said it quite matter-of-factly, as if he was suggesting they might all sit down and have a nice cup of tea after their hour of rolling around on the floor of the stable.

"What?"

Rob had his hand on Matty's back and Matty felt him freeze.

"You heard me." Marchant's voice was steady. "You're going to have to off me, old chap. I can't see any other way to finish it. They didn't seem to think there was any other way, either."

He didn't state who the mysterious *they* were.

Matty lifted his head with an effort and looked at him.

"Cutting the link itself is difficult and if you're successful, there's a strong possibility we both die. Or...if only one of us dies, or is killed, the link dies too, and the other man survives. Finish it, Curland!" Marchant's voice was abrupt. "I'm sick of it. It's been years. I don't want it anymore and there's been enough death. Finish it! Do it now!"

Rob looked at him. He looked back at Matty. Matty shook his head, unable to speak through both nausea and fear. He stood slowly from his position beside Matty and stepped over to where Marchant knelt.

"The book said *exsanguinate*," he said.

"Cut my throat, then," the other man replied matter-of-factly. "Do it, Curland, bloody do it!"

Rob moved around behind him and put a hand in his hair. Matty saw his fingers tighten slowly as he tilted Marchant's head back and exposed his throat. The knife was still open in his other hand, blood already visible on the good steel blade.

He'd had the knife for years. Matty's father had bought it for him when he turned fifteen, Matty remembered. Rob kept it sharp. He used it for everything from cutting twine to gutting rabbits.

He laid it across Marchant's throat.

Marchant met Matty's eyes. "I'm sorry, Webber. It wasn't me who began it, but I should have made more effort to finish it years ago. I should have made the Ternants finish it. I was scared."

He shut his eyes.

Gently, almost reverently, Rob drew the sharp blade of the knife across his neck under his ear. He and Marchant were both deathly silent.

The blood began to well against Marchant's pale skin and spurt over Rob's hand where it remained on his throat.

One of them let out a sigh.

Rob sank to his knees behind Marchant, letting the knife fall as he guided the man back across his lap. His face was blank.

Matty couldn't move. He wanted to go over to them, but weakness kept him resting against the wall. He shut his eyes for a moment and when he opened them, Marchant's head was thrown back and the blood was spurting freely. Rob must have cut his carotid. It was everywhere. They were both covered in it. Rob had slid his arm behind Marchant's head and was holding his hands, where Marchant had them grasped loosely together on his chest.

They were watching each other. Marchant said something. Matty thought he said "It's all right, old chap. It had to be done."

He heard Rob say, "I thought I was done with killing."

Marchant said, "Don't think of it like that. Think of it as saving Webber." And they both turned their heads and looked at him. Marchant looked peaceful. Rob looked tortured.

Matty couldn't bear it.

"Stop!" he said. "Stop the bleeding!" He dragged himself across the floor into the lake of blood and shoved his hands into the middle of it all, over the place it was pumping out. He knew how to do this; he'd done it a few times in France. "I don't bloody well want this, the pair of you! Stop it. Stop bleeding, you bastard!"

He looked up from where he was bent over Marchant, up to Rob. Rob's eyes were still glazed. There was nobody home. Matty slapped him across his cheek with a blood-soaked hand.

"Snap out of it, Rob! Help me!"

Rob tugged at his ear, still not quite with it. Matty hit him again. There was blood all over his face now, as well as all over his chest and lap. "Rob! Help me! I need you to help me!"

And then Rob was back. "Shitfire," he said. "Are you sure?"

"Of course I'm bloody sure, Rob! I'm not going to let you have this on your conscience. Now help me stop the bleeding!"

Marchant was pretty out of it, not gone completely, but certainly away with the fairies. Matty tugged him off Rob's lap completely, pulled his own jacket off and wadded it up, cotton-lining out. He pressed it against the cut.

"Go and get the doctor," he said to Rob. "It's going to need to be stitched. And his hand."

Rob stared at him for a moment. "Rob! God! Go!" Matty shouted and then the other man shot to his feet and was moving. Matty shouted after him "Get her to bring a transfusion kit if she has one!" Marchant was going into shock.

Matty was suddenly feeling more alive than he had for months. He knew he was Type O blood; he'd been stuck full of needles on behalf of the wounded of his platoon several times at the Front. He could spare some blood for Marchant if

Marchant needed it. Marchant had been prepared to give his life to save Matty's. He pressed harder on the bundled-up jacket.

IT WAS THE LONGEST hour of his life before Rob came back with the doctor. Matty had managed to stop the bleeding, but he didn't know if it was soon enough.

Dr Marks was about the same age as Rob, sensible and kept up with the latest medical papers. She was also wearing knickerbockers, which made Matty look twice.

"What?" she said, irritably, as she knelt beside him in the pool of blood without a flinch. "I was about to go for a bicycle ride. Lucky for your young friend here I hadn't left and that I had the car outside. Here. Let me see." She pushed his hands out of the way. "Well, you've stopped it, which is something. But whether he's lost too much..." She trailed off, thinking. "I've brought a transfusion kit...my brother sent me one last year, most interesting..."

As her voice ran out, Matty said, "I'm Type O. I can donate if you can set it up. I've done it before."

She was obviously thinking furiously.

"I haven't," she said, finally. "I've only seen photographs. But I suppose we'll manage." She looked up at Rob. "The kit, Curland?" she said.

"Here, Ma'am," he said, stepping forward. He had been hovering in the doorway as if he was afraid to come in, and he returned there once he'd handed off the wooden box.

She didn't spare him another glance, turning back to Matty. "Roll your sleeve up, then," she said. "It's probably going to hurt. It's a bloody big needle."

"I'll do me, you do him," Matty said, gesturing at Marchant, and she nodded.

He pushed his own sleeve up above his elbow and tied the strap off round his bicep, while the doctor pushed Marchant's sodden sleeve back to reveal his forearm. She muttered to herself under her breath as she did so.

"Right then," she said, once his arm was exposed. "No point putting the line into him before the blood's out of you."

Matty winced as she said the word *line* and saw Rob do the same out of the corner of his eye. "Is he still breathing?" he asked, as she began to pat his inner elbow to raise the veins.

"Don't want to waste your blood on him if he's not?" she asked, acerbically. "Yes, he's still breathing. Heartbeat's faint, though. Are you ready?"

She stuck him with the needle before he could say yes.

The familiar dropping dizziness as the blood drained out of him into the glass vessel was like an old friend. He'd never minded doing it, it was an easy way to help people. A little blood went a long way, both inside and outside the body.

"I should be lying down," he said, vaguely.

"Be my guest." She gestured to the blood-soaked earth of the stable floor.

He coughed in surprise as she neatly pressed down on his vein and slid out the needle. He'd forgotten she had a dark sense of humour.

She bent his hand back up toward his shoulder. "Here. Keep pressure on that." She turned toward Rob.

"Curland! I need you to hold this!" She busied herself putting the top on the glass flask and attaching the tubing. "You're going to turn it upside down so I can get the air out, I'm going to insert the needle, attach the tubing, and then you're going to hold it up for me."

Rob was motionless in the doorway.

"Come on, man. Hurry up! Unless you want him to die?"

Rob shook himself at that and stepped forward. "I don't want him to die," he said, almost to himself.

"Well then. Let's get a chivvy on!"

THE TROUBLE WITH DR Marks, her patients sometimes said, was that once you invited her in, it was almost impossible to get rid of her. She had an extremely strong interest in the wellbeing of people who had asked for her help and she didn't simply let her cases drop willy-nilly once she'd become involved in them.

This proved to be true in all instances.

"Let's get him up to the house then, chaps," she said, as she tied off the sutures she'd used to close the neat, deep, three-inch gash Rob had sliced into the side of Marchand's neck.

Neither of them responded.

Rob was in the doorway to where he had retreated as soon as she'd taken the bottle of blood back from him and Matty had continued kneeling beside her and Marchant on the floor, trying and mostly failing to be of assistance. He felt light-headed but the previously incapacitating nausea and pain in his stomach had disappeared.

"Chaps?" She stood, brushing perfunctorily at her knicker-bockers. It didn't do much good. All four of them were soaked in Marchant's blood.

"Will he live?" Rob's voice was soft and empty, and she eyed him gravely.

"Probably. If he didn't lose too much, if the transfusion doesn't go wrong and didn't get contaminated somehow, and if no-one tries to cut his throat again."

She paused and into the speaking silence again command-ed severely, "Now. Gentlemen. Shall we get him up to the house?"

Matty went and fetched one of the blankets from the aban-doned men's sleeping quarters over the barn. They were folded up neatly in the oak chest in the corner where his mother had arranged it and when he drew out the one on top, it smelled faintly of cedar and lavender, scattered in there against the moths.

He shook it out and brought it down the worn wooden stairs and they doubled it over and rolled Marchant on to it as gently as they could. It wasn't anything either of them lacked experience in.

Then, as the doctor gathered up her precious transfusion kit, they took two corners each and carefully carried him through the rain and up to the house.

"Put him on the table a minute," Dr Marks said, brushing water from her hair as they entered the kitchen. I want to check and see if he has any other wounds."

Rob seemed more himself now he'd had something to do other than stand and stare, and he handed her a towel for her hair. "He doesn't," he said before filling the kettle and putting it on and then turning back to the sink to scrub his hands clean with the carbolic. "Only his hand. As you can see."

"I'll be the judge of that, shall I?" She moved him gently to the side and took up position beside him. "Me being the actual doctor in the room and all that. Pass the soap, please. And if you could put my transfusion kit in to soak, I'd be very grateful."

Rob handed her the soap mutely and Matty suddenly decided he needed to get off his feet. He pulled out one of the kitchen chairs and sat down heavily. She looked at him sharply. "All right?" she asked.

"Bit dizzy," he said. "But yes, I think so."

"You need some tea. Curland here can make some while I check over the patient. What's his name again?"

"Marchant. Peter Marchant. He was a friend of Arthur's."

She sniffed. "Was he now. Well. Let's get his clothes off him, I need to see if he's bleeding anywhere else."

"*He's not!*" Rob's raised voice echoed all around the kitchen as he slammed the brown pottery teapot down on the wooden draining board.

They both stopped still and stared at him. He was holding the handle of the teapot in his hand. It was detached from the pot.

"I'm sorry, Ma'am." He breathed in through his nose, obviously trying to regain precarious control. Matty wanted to go to him but he could tell from the way Rob was holding himself that he'd be pushed away. "He's not bleeding anywhere else. He wasn't— I... It was me." He swallowed. "I cut him."

She stared at him.

"I *beg* your pardon?"

He stared at her and then glanced frantically at Matty, over to Marchant, and then back at her. "I...it was me."

"No. I attacked him first," came an almost inaudible slurred voice from the head of the table. "I attacked him, and he defended himself." Marchant stirred weakly and Dr Marks whipped around and stepped up to him.

"Try not to move around too much," she said, briskly. "I don't want you to start bleeding again." She conjured a pair of scissors from somewhere and began to cut off his shirt. "Stay still. I need to examine you and these clothes need burning."

Marchant made a weak sort of noise and did as he was asked. Or he might have passed out again. He hadn't opened his eyes at all.

"*We will talk about this,*" she said, pinning Rob with gimlet eyes. "But first, I need to stitch this gash on his hand," she glared at the offending appendage as if she held it personally responsible for its injury, "and then we need to get this man into a proper bed and we all need to wash."

WITH MARCHANT PASSED out upstairs after a perfunctory sponge down that Matty and Dr Marks performed between them, and a similar perfunctory wash undertaken by everyone else, each of them without assistance, they settled down around the table in the kitchen. Matty rubbed at the blood that had smudged on to it from Marchant in a desultory fashion with a wet cloth and was slightly surprised to find it left no traces. He'd half expected it to be a permanent stain.

He felt better with a clean table, clean clothes, clean hands and face, and a cup of sweet tea inside him. Luckily his mother had had more than one teapot.

Rob still wasn't right. He was back with them, but his silence was tense and stiff, not his usual comfortable confidence.

"Now," said Dr Marks, in the quiet, firm voice she used with children when she did their inoculations, "will one of you please tell me what the hell is going on?"

"Dr Marks..." Matty didn't know where to start and she interrupted, anyway.

"Sylvia, please. And you are Matthew. And you are Robert. Yes?" She gathered up both their gazes. "Start at the beginning. Not today. Start with what was wrong with your brother, please, Matthew."

Matty swallowed and stared at her.

"What?" he said.

At the same time as Rob said, "You said it was cancer, probably. Liver cancer."

"Yes, I did, didn't I? And it might have been. But I don't think it was, was it?"

She looked from one of them to the other with her head tilted to one side, like a particularly insightful bird. A goose, probably. Or a buzzard. Something that was on the attack, anyway.

Matty broke first. "Not as such, no. We don't think so."

There was a long pause.

She coughed, delicately, and put her cup down in its blue willow-pattern saucer. Matty had got the good china out for her. "Was it magic, Matthew?"

Rob choked on his tea.

By the time Matty had finished thumping him on the back and mopping up the spilt liquid and re-filling everyone's cups, they had both settled a bit.

"Was it magic?" she repeated.

"I don't think they like you to call it that," Rob said, quietly. "As I understand it."

She gave him an assessing look. "No, I don't suppose they do," she said, eventually. "I don't know much about it, really. But I do know that. Tell me."

By the time they had given her an outline, they were on their third pot of tea and she had been up to check on the sleeping Marchant twice. It was getting on for tea-time and the evening was drawing in. The injured man didn't have a temperature and seemed to be sleeping peacefully.

"And did this cut the line?" she asked Matty, finally. "Was it enough? Or are you still connected to him?"

Matty stopped and thought. He hadn't checked since that dreadful moment in the stable as he'd watched Rob get ready to slice Marchant's willing throat.

Rob looked at him from squinted eyes. "It's gone," he said, finally. "I think it's gone."

"You can sense it?" Dr Marks...Silvia...asked. "You're one of them?"

She didn't sound entirely friendly.

Rob pulled at his ear uncomfortably. "No. No, I'm not. Do I *look* like one of them?" he said, irritably. "I tried a few things in the books, that's all, and some of them worked."

"What do you mean, do you look like one of them?" she asked. She was exceedingly sharp. They'd skirted round the bit about Lin of the Frem and the gate between the worlds, concentrating on the line linking Matty, and presumably Arthur before him, to Marchant and how their efforts to cut it had caused Marchant to appear out of thin air.

"Erm…" Rob was all out of hedging ability.

Matty said, quite calmly, "There's a whole other world beyond the shimmer thing that the not-magicians draw power from and there are people who are tall and slim and who carry swords and use magic like you or I use a knife and fork. No, I don't know anything more than that. Yes, I think that's where Marchant was. Yes, let's ask him when he wakes up."

He took a breath. She didn't appear to have anything to say, which was a bloody first.

"What did *you* mean?" he asked, before she could get going again. "*Is Rob one of them?*"

"I only meant…can he do it? That's all." She sounded unsure, which was the first time in all the years he'd known her that he'd heard her sound less than a hundred percent certain about anything, ever. "Like Arthur could."

There was another silence.

Clearly, they had all been hoarding information.

Rob cleared his throat. "Like Arthur could?" he repeated.

"Yes. I'm not a fool, Robert Curland, despite being in skirts. I knew there was something odd about what was wrong with him when he wouldn't let me examine him. He wasn't like the old country boys, who don't like a woman seeing their naked chest outside the bedroom."

Rob blushed and Matty snorted painfully through his nose despite his exhausted misery.

"Annie Beelock asked me to come out and see him one Saturday morning when I saw her in the post office. She said he was lethargic, not eating, and she was worried about him. She couldn't persuade him to come down to the surgery, so I called in as I was passing by on my way home." She proffered the teapot at Matty and he shook his head as she refilled her own cup. "I could see him through the sitting room window." She put the teapot down with a decisive little thump. "He was waving his arms around and there was a cloud of light in the room with him."

There was a potent silence.

"What did you do?" Rob asked, eventually, when it seemed as if she had run out of words.

"I watched for a while, obviously. What would you have done?" It was a rhetorical question. "And then when he seemed to have finished whatever he was doing and the light had gone away, I knocked on the door and asked him to tell me what he was up to."

There was another pause. She was an astonishing woman.

"And what did he say?" It was Matty's turn to prompt her.

"He said he'd found a book of instructions about how to make things happen with an invisible power, it absolutely wasn't magic, how I dare I call it that, and that he was going to create a weapon to end the war and bring the boys home."

A heavy silence fell over all three of them.

"That's what he told me he was doing, too," said Marchant, in an exhausted whisper, from the doorway.

They all leapt out of their collective skins.

He was leaning against the door jamb and the trip down the stairs had clearly been unwise. He was a pale greenish colour and looked done in.

"Sit!" barked the doctor. "Idiot!" Her bedside manner was dreadful.

She jumped to her feet along with Matty and they guided him down into the carver chair with arms at the head of the table. He folded down bonelessly, breathing quick and shallow and shut his eyes, resting his head on the tall ladder-back. The movement exposed the dressing Sylvia had put on his neck and Matty caught Rob staring at it, almost transfixed.

"Pour him some tea, would you Rob?" Matty asked, hoping to distract him. "I expect he could do with a drink."

"He shouldn't even be out of bed," Sylvia said.

"I could hear you talking," Marchant rasped. "I wanted to tell my part of it."

"Drink your tea." Rob's voice was quiet as he put the mug down on the table in front of him.

"Thank you." He looked up at Rob. "I'm sorry, Curland. I shouldn't have asked it of you."

Rob turned away and busied himself filling the kettle, stoking up the range and finding more milk.

"It's all right," he said finally, soft country voice that of the real Rob again. "I know what it's like. That just wanting it all to be over. I was stuck under a collapsed building for hours once, waiting for it to fall. It would have almost been a relief if it had." He ran a hand through his already-disordered hair as he turned back to them. "And it was enough, as it turns out. Unless you can still feel it?"

Marchant's eyes were shut again, and he took a little while to answer. "No," he said. "I think it's gone. Whatever we did, between us, it's gone. Arthur began it years ago and it looks like we've finished it today."

His part of the story didn't take all that long to tell, but it wasn't comfortable listening. Matty had always looked up to Arthur. This didn't sound like the Arthur he knew.

"He really wasn't well, toward the end, before you came home," Sylvia told him. "In his mind, I mean, as well as physically. He certainly thought he was going to make a weapon so terrible it would end the war. Annie was truly worried about him the day she asked me to come out here."

"His letters to me got more and more rambling," Marchant added. "I'm not sure they'd have made sense even before the censor got to them." He drank some of his tea. "Is the war over?" he asked, cautiously. "I don't even know what date it is."

"It's two days before Christmas, 1919," Matty told him. "And you should probably go back to bed. If you feel half as bad as you look, you're dead on your feet." He stood up. "Plus, none of us had any lunch and it's nearly tea-time. I am going to have some bread and cheese and fruit cake. You may all have some too if you would like some, but even if you don't, I'm still going to." He moved decisively toward the larder.

He didn't want to hear any more about Arthur going mad this evening. He'd had enough for one day.

CHAPTER NINE: An Ending and a Beginning

Marchant mostly slept the next day. He'd drunk a cup of sweet tea and eaten half a slice of toast, then they'd manhandled him back up the stairs into bed and the doctor...Sylvia...had taken her leave in her little car after the three of them had consumed a respectable amount of bread, cheese, and fruitcake.

"I'm going to leave him to your tender mercies, Mr Curland," she had said to Rob, rinsing out her blood transfusion equipment in the sink as she prepared to leave. Matty had gone to bring her car round to the front of the house from the yard. "You broke him. You can fix him." She shot him a sidelong glance as he flinched. "Joking, Robert. I was joking." She put the glass vessel on the wet draining board and turned toward him, reaching across him to get the tea-towel from where it hung on the rail in front of the range. There was a short silence as she dried off her paraphernalia and tucked it neatly in the wooden box next to him on the table.

He watched her hands as she packed it all away. Short, blunt competent fingers that soothed and healed and repaired.

Unlike his own, laid on the table palm down before him. His were used more for destroying and killing now.

She shut the case and latched it shut with a little huff of satisfaction and then turned the chair next to him, so it faced him and sat down on it. She reached out one of her healing hands and placed it over his killing one. "Robert," she said, quietly. "Look at me."

He did as she asked. He didn't have much option really. She was so stubborn she'd simply sit there until he did as she asked.

Her eyes were dark with sympathy. "Rob," she said. "I think you need to let it go."

He swallowed. "Not sure I can," he said. He didn't bother to dissemble and ask what she meant. "I cut the man's throat, Sylvia."

"And extremely cleanly, too," she said, patting his hand as if congratulating him. "If you'd made a messier job of it, he'd be dead. It was clinically neat." She patted his hand again. "A mercy blow, if you like."

"Sylvia..." He swallowed.

"You were trying to save Matthew's life. Marchant gave you permission to do it. Begged you, as I understand it." She paused a moment to allow him to cast his mind back. "It wasn't much of a choice now, was it?"

He shook his head dumbly.

"Kill the man asking you for a mercy blow in order to save the man you..." Her voice trailed off. "That's not a choice, Robert. That's no choice at all."

She left her hand where it was for a little while. It was warm and reassuring and he took comfort from it.

"I know," he said, finally. And after a while, "I'd do anything for Matty."

"Yes," she said quietly. "It's easy to see, if you know." She patted his hand again. "Don't worry, Rob. I would bet a considerable amount that Marchant is going to be fine, particularly if he can stay here for a bit and be looked after. And I think you've done him a favour by bringing him back from wherever he was. The Outlands, he called it?"

Rob nodded. "Yes, that's what they call it."

"He didn't seem to like it much," she said. "From the little he said before he needed to rest."

"He was a prisoner," Rob said.

"Well then," she said, practically. "You helped him as well. I'll try not to make jokes about it from now on, though." She patted his hand and withdrew her own as she spoke.

"I'd appreciate it," he said. "I would really appreciate it." He stood as she rose and hefted her case. "Let me take that," he offered.

She smiled and passed it to him. "I'll be back tomorrow to check on him. You should get the telephone out here, you know. It would have saved you running all that way. Although why you didn't take the car I don't know."

"I forgot," he said. "I plain forgot that we have it. I'm a fool in more ways than one."

She looked at him shrewdly. "I don't think so, Robert. I don't think so at all." She patted his arm reassuringly. "There's Matthew with the car. Come on."

IT WAS ABOUT SIX IN the evening on Christmas Day when Marchant decided he'd had enough and took himself back to bed. He'd spent the day before mostly asleep.

Sylvia had come and checked on him at dinner time—and had joined them at the table in the kitchen when she saw Mrs Beelock serving thick slices of home-cured ham with kale and boiled potatoes. "Just in time!" she'd declared happily before sitting down arms akimbo as if she hadn't eaten for a week. "I always forget what a good table you keep, Annie!"

Annie Beelock harrumphed a little at her. "You're a flatter-er, Sylvia Marks, and you always have been. Here." She put a filled plate down in front of her. "And you might as well come to dinner tomorrow as well if you've got nowhere else to go. I'm serving up and then going home to Bert and you can help them wash up." She was smiling when she turned back toward the range to pick up another warm plate to fill.

"I'd be delighted, thank you so much for the invitation." She smiled at Matty. "It's extremely kind of you, Matthew!"

Matty laughed. "You're always welcome, Sylvia. Come after church."

Marchant was still worryingly weak, but he'd made it downstairs to join them for Christmas dinner, although he hadn't eaten much. Then he'd laid on the settee in the sitting room and dozed on and off whilst the three of them sat and reminisced in front of the fire, nursing glasses of brandy. Naturally the talk turned to Arthur and the books. It was hard to get away from them...they were stacked up in piles all around the room.

"Are you going to keep doing it?" Sylvia asked Rob at one point. "Are you going to teach yourself more?"

Rob hesitated. "Part of me wants to," he answered. "I'd like to learn more about it. But it seems like it's very easy to get it wrong. Fatally."

Marchant stirred where he was lying under the rug and joined in the conversation. "It *is* singularly easy to get it wrong," he said. He hadn't spoken much during dinner. He'd eaten some of the goose and a few sprouts and then given his apologies, saying that was all he could manage. But he hadn't wanted to go back to bed yet and Rob had handed him in here to rest.

The three of them looked over at him. He didn't sit up, but he turned on his side so he could see them. "Arthur got it really wrong," he said. "And on the other side...they're dangerous people. You met one, didn't you?" He looked from Matty to Rob.

Matty blushed and Rob found his own face heating. They hadn't told Sylvia much about Lin.

"Yes," Rob admitted. "Lin. Of the Frem. How did you know?"

"He was...not a friend exactly. But friendly. As much as he could be." He brushed a hand over his face, shutting his eyes briefly. "He said that he'd been here, that you'd helped him shut a gate someone had opened in the shimmer."

Sylvia's eyes were wide. "A gate?"

"Yes." Matty was matter of fact. "Behind the barn. It's gone now. Whatever Lin did, it disappeared, and we're damned sure it didn't come back. We keep checking. There were...things. Carnas, he called them. Screaming."

"Carnas," Marchant confirmed. "They call them carnas. They use them to police the shimmer and make sure it stands between their world and ours. They're..." He shuddered and looked a bit sick. "Absolutely vile-looking. And dangerous." He pushed himself up to sitting and wrapped his arms around his drawn-up legs, leaning against the back of the wide settee and rearranging the blanket to his satisfaction, addressing his words to his knees.

"If you pull too much energy from the shimmer as you're working, it thins, and they can get through. I don't really understand it. They didn't tell me much about the mechanics of it. But it's definitely dangerous. Using kias...that's what they call it...is dangerous." Matty nodded in agreement. "I can do a bit. They had me shut in a room by myself a lot of the time. I didn't have much else to do." He pulled a face. "I'm not sure I'd like to do it here, though. Not without one of them around to back me up." He looked at them. "They're a lot more powerful than they look. They're strong physically, but that's not all there is to them—they're supremely powerful workers. They have much more innate kias than most humans. Lin and I talked about it a bit."

He brushed he hands over his face again. "I'm getting tired. I need to go back to bed I think."

"I'll give you a hand," Rob said. "Come on." He rose to help him, and Sylvia Marks rose too.

"Let's have a look at that dressing once you're upstairs, Mr Marchant. It looked like it was healing up well yesterday, but it won't hurt to check."

She had pronounced herself satisfied and departed soon after. He and Matty had taken station in the sitting room again with a large pot of tea accompanying goose and stuffing sandwiches, with cold roast potatoes.

This time they arranged themselves on the sofa where Marchant had been lying, and after they'd eaten they ended up with Rob sitting up, legs stretched out on to the footstool and Matty sprawled along the settee with his head in his lap.

"I don't think I'm ever going to need to eat again," Matty said, after a while. He had his cup and saucer of tea balanced precariously on his middle and had been attempting to drink from it without having to sit up.

"If you spill tea all over my leg like you did the last time you tried that, I'll not be very happy, my lad," Rob warned him. "I'll make sure you won't have the opportunity to eat anything. I can't move away from you if you try it, either, because I'm as stuffed as you are."

Matty finally managed to make the lip of the cup meet his mouth without any disaster and emptied it. "There!" he said triumphantly. "I knew I could do it! Here, put the cup on the floor for me, would you?"

Rob did as he was bid. He was half a second from dozing off, warm and comfortable and trapped under the man he'd been in love with for years.

"So, is that it, then?" Matty asked, after a while. "We tidy the books up nicely, keep them dusted, and forget about it all?"

They sat for a while, watching the fire dance, pondering. Rob found himself absently pushing his fingers through Matty's hair. He didn't have brilliantine on it today and it was soft and fine, falling over his eyes and tangling in his lashes.

Rob didn't, honestly, want to pursue the path he'd started on. His motivation to learn had been to help Matty, rather than to become a user of the power for its own sake. The kias, he corrected himself.

"I think..." he said, hesitantly "...I think I'd like to do just that, if that's all right with you, love. I don't need to do any more with it. We've stopped what was happening to you. And that meant we got Marchant home, without ever knowing he was there. I'm happy with that. It feels like a good place to leave it. And the end of a year feels like a good time to let it rest.

"You and Marchant are both safe. Arthur...he was a fool, Matty. A dangerous fool. I know he was your brother. But still. It's the truth."

Matty nodded in agreement. "I loved him. But yes, in this he was. Like Sylvia said, he wasn't well in his mind."

"A lot of people aren't well in their minds these days...the war has done that to millions, one way or another. And the influenza hasn't helped." His watched his fingers, stroking, stroking, stroking through Matty's hair in the quiet firelight. "I don't want to go that way. I want to live here, with you. A normal life. I want a normal life with you. A get-up-have-breakfast-feed-the-cows sort of life. I'm not keen on being a magician."

Matty gave a small, huffing chuckle. "I'm not exactly keen on it either, if I'm honest. Part of me would like to know more. But...we've been through all these books again and again and we've made as much sense as we can of it all. Perhaps Marchant could make more of them, if he wants to. I agree with you. I want a quiet life. I want to be able to spend my days and nights with you, Rob. We've waited a long time for this. And the last five years have been hell. Let's let it settle. Put the books on the shelf and let it all settle down."

He reached a hand up and cupped Rob's cheek, bringing him down for a brief, soft kiss that Rob couldn't hold for long, not being able to fold himself in half. "If in twelve months you're bored and you decide you do want to learn how to be a magician, maybe Marchant will give you a hand."

It was Rob's turn to laugh. "I think Marchant might be done with it too," he said. "He got thoroughly caught up in it and he knows first-hand how dangerous it is. Another world, though...beyond ours. Imagine!"

"I know," Matty said. "But let's make the most of this one for a bit, shall we?" He pushed himself up on to his elbows, so Rob was able to properly reach his mouth and they let the conversation lapse in favour of quiet, intense kisses in the light of the fire.

THE END

ABOUT A.L. LESTER

Hello there! I live in rural Somerset in the UK, with Mr AL, two children and a variety of other animals. I'm non-binary/pan, I have a seizure disorder that means my life has become a bit cramped in the last few years and one of our children has a very rare life-limiting medical condition. I write and read in the cracks. I like permaculture gardening, knitting small things, reading pretty much anything and making other people laugh. Also, ducks.

All my social media links and more about the Lost in Time universe and my other books are on my website, where you can also sign up for my newsletter: allester.co.uk[1]. There are maps and additional material and I add a bit more stuff whenever I have time.

Thank you for reading! Here's the first bit of *Lost in Time*, in case you haven't seen it.

---

1. http://allester.co.uk/

LOST IN TIME

Prologue: 2016

In a quiet room the glow of the surrounding circle of candles gave off a dim warm light.

He sat cross-legged in silence on the floor in front of the silver bowl of water in the center of the circle, palms open, relaxed, hands on his knees. The surface of the water was still. Very carefully, he reached out a hand and picked up the small bottle on the floor next to him. Equally carefully, he tilted it slowly until a single drop fell into the center of the bowl.

It was oily and it spread out quickly over the surface, shimmering darkly. It smelled of cedar and cypress and pine; green depths and rich earthy expectations; still and dark as the forest from which it had come.

He replaced the lid on the bottle and put it back on the floor.

Steadily, he drew in a breath. It was make or break time now. He either gave up and never came back to this, or he pursued the path he'd been following for the last fortnight.

With resolve, he lifted his hands and placed them on the bowl, cupping it. He began, very, very cautiously, to open up his Othersense, breathing in the scent of the oil, aware of the light of the candles falling on his skin in an almost tactile way and letting his focus narrow down to the center of the ring of flame, dismissing everything else as superfluous.

He closed his eyes and pictured Mira, the sense of her.

Dark, strong, beautiful. Headstrong. Driven. Self-centered. Mercurial. Stubborn.

There. A twist and a push and there it was. A flash, like the edge of a coat or dress disappearing around a corner. A red dress. He rushed after it with his Othersense, grasping, afraid he'd lose it because it was so faint. As he did so he let go of the bowl—it was only a tool to focus anyway—and reached out with hands, as if that would help.

It was faint, faint, faint, and fading. He took a huge breath in, breathed out, and pushed, grabbed for it, caught the trailing edge in his outstretched hand and closed his fingers, both mentally and in reality.

There was a loud bang and shock of cold as the temperature in the room dropped suddenly. All the candles went out at once. He still had his eyes shut but the glow of light on his eyelids was replaced with darkness. He gasped and started coughing as cold, wet air hit his lungs.

Chapter 1: Coming Home, 1918

The empty police office smelled the same. Dusty formality, sweat, exhaustion, and boredom. The sun came in through the high arched windows and turned the dust motes in the air to clouds of golden haze. The dark wooden desks shone and the chairs were in the same positions they had been in four years ago. Even the paperwork piled on the surfaces looked like it hadn't shifted an inch.

Alec stood for a moment in the open doorway and took it all in, re-acclimatizing. He still felt odd in his civvies, even more so now he was back at work. For four years, 'work' had equaled a uniform, webbing, puttees, a Webley revolver on his hip, and a red cap. Now he was in one of his pre-war suits, slightly too small across the shoulders, and an overcoat that smelled of mothballs. He took it off and hung it, with his hat, on the tall umbrella stand by the door.

"Can I help you?" A pleasant, light voice came from behind him as he turned back. A chap leaned in the open doorway on the right of the room, cup and saucer of tea balanced in one hand. He was wearing an immaculately-cut pinstripe suit. Alec immediately felt shabby. He stepped forward, regardless, holding out his hand.

"Good morning. I'm Alastair Carter. The new inspector."

The other man smiled and moved to put his tea down and clasp Alec's hand with a warm, firm grip. "Ah, yes, the Super said you'd be starting today. Will Grant. I'm your sergeant. Very pleased to meet you." He picked his cup up again. "Come and get a cup of tea and I'll show you around. We're rather short-staffed, I'm afraid. There's just me, Laurence, and Percy.

Desperately glad you've arrived. We've been puttering along, but there's plenty to get stuck into."

He busied himself pouring tea from a pot on the desk in the small office he'd emerged from. "I've been in here, but I'll clear out into the main office. It's the Inspector's cubbyhole, actually. You were stationed here before?"

"Yes, for a few months. It's not changed much." He looked around. Vesper had been the inspector in '14. The old man had retired a few months ago, well past the age he should have been pensioned off. During all his time in France Alec had known he'd come back, but he hadn't thought he'd come straight in again as an inspector. They were desperately under-manned though, Wolsey had said yesterday when he'd gone down to Scotland Yard to see him.

Poplar had always been Alec's patch even as a uniformed constable and he was happy to be able to slide back into an area he already knew. It was a distance from his house out at Hampstead, but it was interesting, necessary work that includ-ed the docks and some poor areas he considered in more urgent need of policing than the richer areas to the west of the City of London. He'd been offered a choice between his old station at Wapping and a new start somewhere further west. Of course, he'd chosen Wapping. Being handed a promotion as well was a pleasant and unexpected surprise.

"No hurry to move out just now," he said to Grant. "There's plenty of space for me to settle in around you whilst you shuffle paper. Have you been here long? You weren't here before the war, were you? I don't remember you."

"No, I got a Blighty in '15 and came back here after I got on my feet again. After a fashion. I was only just out of uniform, over in Holborn when I joined up, but they needed the men and I was it, so Detective Sergeant Grant it was." He grimaced ruefully. "We've been doing a lot of learning on the job, but we've managed. A bigger team is a huge relief. And a boss here on site." He coughed apologetically, hand over his mouth. "And someone who can run a hundred yards without expiring."

Alec raised a questioning eyebrow.

"Belgian front," Grant replied, with economy.

"Ah." That had been bad. Alec had seen the results of several gas attacks himself and it would go with him to the grave. It was only too easy to imagine what Grant had gone through both during and after the event. That poet fellow, Owen, had had it down to a tee.

Alec had come across a pamphlet of poems one day a week or two ago, kicking round Bloomsbury waiting for the Met to get back in touch with him. Graphic stuff that had made him even more grateful it was all over. He considered mentioning it to Grant and then thought better of it. He didn't want to get off on the wrong foot with the man. If he was as competent as he was pleasant, there was the makings of a good team here.

Chapter 2: The Beginning, 1919

He was cold. And it was dark. Damp, cold air pulling in and out of his lungs. He was lying down, crumpled against cold, wet concrete or brick. He struggled to open his eyes as he pressed himself back against the wall, driven by a terror he couldn't place as something loomed over him and pushed past. His head was fuzzy, banging with pain, and his body felt like one enormous bruise.

Fear finally drove him to get his eyes open and he relaxed a fraction when he saw he was alone in a small alley, lit only by the hazy glare of a street lamp at the junction with a larger street. He tipped his head back in relief and took a moment to orient himself in the relative safety.

He was unharmed, although his head was pounding and his entire body ached like he had run a marathon or been beaten. But he had no memory of either of those things happening. Bile rose in his throat and he barely had time to fall forward on his hands and knees before he vomited, disgustingly and com-prehensively until dry heaves were all he had left.

He rested for a moment, head hanging, the drizzle spatter-ing over him, before he gathered the strength to push himself back against the wall.

What had happened? His mind was a blank. He shud-dered.

His name was Lew. What was he doing here? How had he got here? His breathing started to reflect his panicky state of mind and he automatically began counting his in-breath, hold-breath, out-breath before he was even conscious of it.

So, his name was Lew, and he knew how to handle himself when he started a panic attack.

Good. That was good. Useful. Because it seemed like a good skill to have at this particular moment in time.

Time. Time...she'd moved through time. That didn't make sense. Who'd moved through time? He focused on his breath-ing again, quietly letting the misty rain settle on his upturned, aching face, trying to pack the panic down deep inside.

There wasn't anything he could get a grip on. Every time he reached out to a foggy picture in his head, it moved further away. Memory was slippery and twisted, like silk rope, looping round and leading nowhere.

Finally, the buzzing in his head subsided enough for him to clamber to his feet—with the support of the wall at his back—and after catching his breath, he thought to check his pockets.

Wallet, cards, money. Phone. He switched it on whilst he went through the wallet.

Driving license—Lewis Rogers, twenty-six years old, place of residence London, England. Qualified to drive any category vehicle up to a 7.5-ton truck. A debit card for Barclays. No credit cards. The driving license and a dog-eared organ donor card agreed his next of kin was Mrs. P. Rogers of Brighton, relationship—Mother.

In his jeans pocket was four pounds and twenty-seven pence in small change; and in his wallet, fifty quid in two twenties and a tenner, that looked as if they'd come straight out of the cash-point.

That triggered a little flurry of memory. He'd got it out on his way home, as it was getting dark, from the cash-point on the corner of Garter Row. There was a Tesco Metro there and he'd got out sixty quid and spent some of it on a loaf of bread and some milk. The face of the check-out girl came back to him, her dark hair winging across her eyes as she smiled and handed him his change. He'd shoved it in his pocket, along with the receipt.

His phone had booted and he checked it. No signal. Typical.

It was still drizzling, the kind of fine cloud of almost-mist that drenched through clothes in no time.

He drew a breath and started to scroll down his list of contacts—splinters and flashes of memory coming back to him as he did so. Regan, a tall blond with a curling Celtic tattoo over his right bicep. Mark, a laughing face in a pub somewhere, after rugby. Katie, a tiny frame, hands dancing as she waved them to illustrate her point. Mira, green eyes and a red dress, a low singing voice crooning an old song...

...and with a thump, the weight of memory hit him, like a sock full of sand to the back of his head.

It left him gasping and near to vomiting again, desperately sorting through the shattered splinters of imagery falling into place.

A coherent picture began to emerge as he forced his breath in and out, in and out.

The Border. Capital T. Capital B.

Another chunk of memory fell into place. The Border was a tool he used and a threat he managed. The memory made his entire skin twitch and his hands tingle.

He had been working The Border, he was sure. Looking for what?

Mira. He had been looking for Mira. The mental image of the girl with green eyes and sleek bob popped up again. Mira was lost in the Shadowlands—something had gone wrong while she was Pulling the stuff of The Border to her will. She shouldn't have been doing it.

The Border was power, contained in a matrix no one he had ever spoken to even pretended to understand—they knew it was power, it was danger, it could be worked with; and it should not be misused for your own ends because there was no knowing what would happen. It could quickly leap out of your control, perhaps for its own purpose, perhaps manipulated by those who lived on the other side.

They didn't know enough about it to do, safely, more than Pull a little of the stuff of it to repair where it seemed to be thinning and to use it for small Workings to make life a little easier.

And Mira had wanted more. She had found...His memory stuttered again, too much too soon...a book...a book of rituals? A book of spells? His mind revolted against the description, but that was what she'd called it. She hadn't shown it to him, although he'd seen a few pages of it open on her table after he had broken into her flat to search for her; and he had tried to mimic what she had seemed to have done with it.

She had told him she knew how to use the spells inside it.

He'd laughed at her words. His father, the person who had taught him what little he knew, would have scoffed at the word 'spell.' He had talked of Pulling and Working. Mira though...She wanted to manipulate the tangible fabric Lew had dedicated his entire existence to balancing, to smoothing, blocking the holes and gaps that appeared. She wanted to use it for her own ends.

Lew had told her to be careful. That his experience, and that of the people who had taught him, had made him fear the consequences of trying to take a lot of power for oneself and form it to one's own will. But Mira was confident she could handle it. She had wanted the new job so badly she simply hadn't listened.

Lew had had to break down her door to get in. He had felt the Pull of her Working from his flat a couple of miles away—it had been so visceral, so strong. He'd rushed to her flat as soon as he could, but she was gone. The candles had still been burning. The book was open at a handwritten page; instructions for getting the job or work you wanted.

He had no idea what had happened then. His memory told him he had put all possible wards and guards in place before he undertook his search for her a fortnight later; and he had blocked all the loopholes he could think of that might open up and allow anything to ooze through from behind The

Border. He had made his ritual as concise and tightly formed as he possibly could, to give less chance of errors.

So, where the hell was he?

THERE WAS NO ONE ELSE about—the alley was deserted. He made his way slowly toward the entrance and realized he was near the river, probably downstream a bit, where there were still warehouses. That explained why it was so quiet. He put it to his back and started walking toward what he assumed was the

north. He could pick up a cab and get home then, and work out what had happened. His Working must have fritzed out somehow—unsurprising given what he'd been trying to do.

The streetlights were out and the clouds and drizzle made it even darker. So much so he didn't see the two men until they stepped out in front of him. He went to move around them, sluggishly, but they were too quick, grabbing him by his arms and slamming him in to the wall. He fought back in a desultory fashion, but he was still too dizzy to defend himself properly.

They took his wallet and left him gasping on the ground again with a final punch to the solar plexus. He still had his phone though, that was something. If only he could get signal. He checked again. Not even a bar to call 999.

Finally there were streetlights and one or two people passed him, giving him a wide berth—he probably had a black eye by now and he knew he was limping. Nowhere looked familiar. He kept walking north-east, toward what should be the center of town.

It was all unfamiliar. A couple of vintage cars passed him.

Was there a rally or something going on? He didn't remember seeing anything advertised. Everyone was well bundled up against the rain, heads down, hurrying to get home or to work. He realized it was starting to get light—dawn was breaking. Shouldn't it be busier? It wasn't even a Sunday for it to be this quiet.

Finally, he hit an open newsagent and fumbled in his pocket for some change. Perhaps they'd let him use their phone and he could ring for a cab. As he was standing outside, his eye caught the stack of papers for sale. The headline screamed "Mrs. Astor elected as MP" in large letters. The date at the top read "29 November 1919."

Slowly, he put his change back in his pocket and stepped back a little. He put his shoulder to the damp wall and breathed quietly, taking in his surroundings in a way he hadn't before.

The clothes. The cars. The horses. The hats. The hats gave it away. Everyone had a hat. Caps, tall homburgs, the occasional bowler. All the women with different headgear. The hemlines. The boots. Everyone had boots on.

He was starting to attract attention. He felt sick. He stumbled down another side alley and crouched in a deserted doorway and tried to gather his thoughts.

He was sure he was in London. The one or two voices he had heard, muted by the rain, gave it away if nothing else, but he hadn't yet placed where he was. He put aside how this had happened, he needed to work out how to deal with the consequences. No wonder his phone couldn't get signal. He got it out of his pocket and turned it off. No point.

His inventory was lacking. Phone. A few coins. The clothes on his back. Nothing else. What the hell was he going to do?

IN THE END, HE WALKED and walked. Getting out of the city seemed like a good idea, rather than being picked up as a vagrant. Sleeping rough and stealing food from bins was a bad way to live. He stole an overcoat from a man in a café. It had had a few coins in the pocket and he was able to afford a bit of food. He put aside the thought he was now a thief.

His vague idea he would be safer if he got himself out of London and found somewhere to hide, away from people, led him to Harlow, following the main road east out of the city.

Going over the bridge at Harlow he came head to head with a bloke on a motorbike, going too fast around the sharp corner. The biker braked hard and slid sideways on the icy road. The man went headlong into the river, head and neck already at an odd angle

from the way he'd hit the road under the fallen machine.

Lew ended up tangled under the bike too. He lay there in a distressed heap, legs trapped, feeling the exhaust burning against his calf. Panting and struggling he failed to push it off him.

HIS MEMORY WAS JUMBLED, like a dream. He could remember being tangled with the bike, in the ditch. He was muzzy, couldn't remember how he got there—a recurring theme in his recent life, he thought ruefully. The bike's engine had cut out, which was a relief; but it was on top of his leg, which was painful.

Then his memories came back with a thud.

He was stuck in 1919 and it was raining. It seemed to always be raining in 1919. He remembered it wasn't his bike he was stuck under; and then there was a man shouting at him from the road, which seemed odd, as earlier there was only him and the biker; and he was fairly sure, from the way the biker had been hurling toward the water, there would be no shouting from him.

He'd jumped into the ditch to avoid the bike. Good. That made sense of his immediate situation, if not the shouting man. He could smell petrol, which wasn't all that great.

The shouting stopped after a while, which was nice. Then the bike was moved, which was initially excruciatingly painful, but much better once it was no longer pressing into his knee.

Then unstoppable hands were patting him down and pulling him to his feet, a relentless shoulder was pushed under his arm, and he was hauled without ceremony up to the road again.

"What happened, did you take the corner too fast?

Coming up there to the bridge is a bit sharp."

He didn't answer, fighting to catch his breath against the pain in his leg, and his good Samaritan continued, "No, no, don't try to talk. We've got you. Not a good night to be out in it, at all. On your way back home?" There was a pause for breath and then, "Good grief, man, let's have a look at that leg."

Then there were more flashes of memory; the recollection of being pulled into a car and a woman's voice saying, "That's it, Mac, he's in. I'm worried about his leg, let's get him to Grimes's and then worry about his 'cycle. We can send Grimes's man back for it."

And the man saying, "Mind his head, he's smashed it properly."

Then it all went mercifully dark for a bit.

His next clear recollection was of an old-fashioned doctor's surgery, where he seemed to be lying on a leather couch. An older man with impressive side-whiskers was bent over his leg. The trousers that had covered the leg had disappeared.

Disturbing, but he passed out again before he could query it.

Buy Lost in Time: https://allester.co.uk/find-books/

CPSIA information can be obtained
at www.ICGtesting.com
Printed in the USA
BVHW030442260420
578277BV00001B/113